A Prophecy's End

Wind of Destiny, Volume Three

AJ Cooper

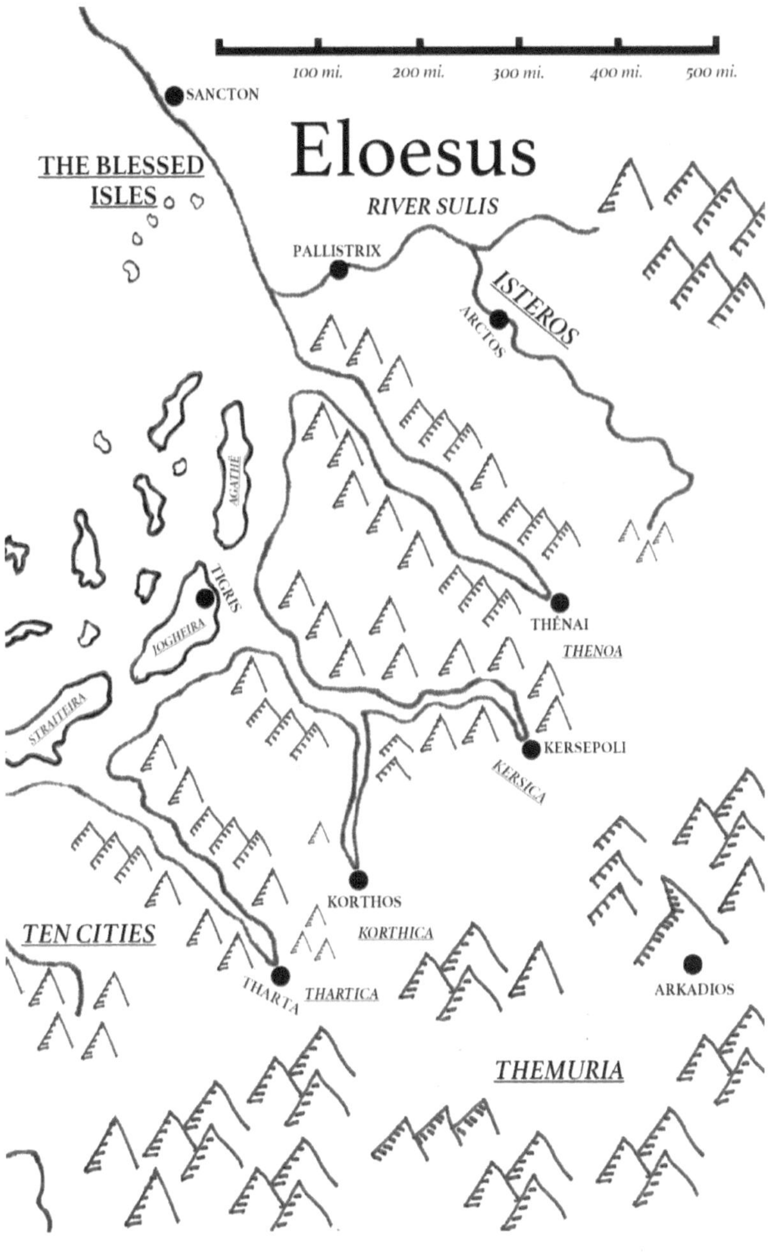
100 mi.
200 mi.
300 mi.
400 mi.
500 mi.
SANCTON
Eloesus
THE BLESSED ISLES
RIVER SULIS
PALLISTRIX
ISTEROS
ARCTOS
AGATHÉ
TIGRIS
JOGHEIRA
STRAITEIRA
THÉNAI
THENOA
KERSEPOLI
KERSICA
KORTHOS
KORTHICA
TEN CITIES
THARTA
THARTICA
ARKADIOS
THEMURIA

THE RIDER IN BLACK

The stamping feet were so numerous, marching through the wilderness, that the deafening sound could be heard in cities miles away, along the seashore. In the twisted brush, in the baking hot sun, rivers once had pierced the barrenness but they had been drunk dry, leaving the streambed below.

At the front of the expedition, led by horsemen and a range of cavalry, the desert had begun to show signs of fading—small pockets of dense grass and an abundance of dirty watering-holes. Three times, shepherds had fled from the army with their flocks. No doubt they would tell everyone living in the cities of their coming peril. But they could do nothing now; Eloesus' doom was sure.

~

At the far end of the army, forty miles from the front, a rider on a black horse, dressed all in black, had been riding for many hours when finally, the King of Kings' cavalcade was reached. The platform on which the King of Kings rode was massive and heavy, with giant wheels grinding across the barren desert. Pulling it were not horses or oxen but a team of two-hundred slaves, captives from Khazidea and Ten Cities, Molkoro and all the far corners of the world. They were attached to the rolling platform by chains and iron handles which they pushed. Their bodies—white, red, brown and black—glistened with sweat. At the first sight of hesitation or laziness the driver—a giant Khand in a white turban—would crack his whip.

The rider removed her hood, revealing the wizened face of Bat Zor.

"My queen!" cried the Khand. Immediately, he screamed

"Stop!"

The slaves stopped their pulling, taking this precious moment to catch their breaths. A chain reaction followed—the legion of elephants immediately ahead stopped their march at the behest of their mahouts. When the King of Kings stopped, everyone stopped.

Bat Zor despised this heat. Yet it was nothing compared to what she had experienced as a girl, in Shakrath. She dismounted from her horse Zara. The poor beast was undernourished and dehydrated. Yet she had survived worse. She was strong, a Megiddi horse used to the dryness and heat of the desert. Old Zara had been bought as a birthday present at an incredible cost; she had been the best of the breed.

Bat Zor gathered her courage, said a short prayer to Bel-Nohai and began ascending the platform's steps. Approaching her husband without request was dangerous enough; to bring him bad news bordered on foolish.

Two Rephathite guards, tall and fair-complexioned, wearing skirts of mail and bearing greatswords and shields, did not stir from their duty as she passed them by. Anyone else besids her would have been cut down on the stone steps.

~

Her husband the King of Kings was hidden from her by a cloth veil. It was said that if a man or woman of low birth viewed his face, they would be stricken dead. Yet Bat Zor had seen his face beyond the veil; she had seen him unclothed. She had borne him a daughter—the cause of all their troubles. There was no true love between Bat Zor and the King of Kings, only duty. Love was for Eloesian goatherds; fear was for the King of Kings' chief wife.

She knelt down before the veil. She could not help but

notice her old hands were trembling. She thought of her innate powers, her abilities to shape people's wills and emotions. She had never dared to use it on her husband, so great was her fear of him. Magi and sorcerers had power over fire, water and air; but who could stand before the King of Kings, who held power over countless millions, over hundreds of nations and great lords. That power, only a god could match. And in the eyes of many, he *was* one.

"My wife," said the King of Kings.

His voice was calm, welcoming. He would not kill her… yet.

"I know your footstep," he said. His voice was deep and carried well wherever it was spoken. "I know your scent."

"I am sorry," said Bat Zor. "I am sorry." She began to weep. The taste of disappointment was recent and bitter. The grief and the fear turned her into a mess of emotion. "I am so sorry, husband…"

"What happened?" said the King of Kings. There still was no anger in his voice. "I am sure whatever it is, it is not your fault."

"Your vizier has been killed," said Bat Zor. "The wicked heathens of Eloesus stabbed him to death. They sold his coat and his headdress. Your beloved Khusruh is dead."

Your daughter joined the rebellion, she had intended to say, but surely such truthful words would invite a beating. She was not ready to speak the truth yet. She was not ready to let him know. For Zubeida's rebellion, the King of Kings would blame her. She blamed herself. A better mother would not have raised such a wicked child. A good Shakrathite mother instilled fear into her children, a fear that never left them even into adulthood.

"They will pay," said the King of Kings with exemplary calmness and confidence. "They will regret everything when their fields are burning… when their temples are ruined… when their people are taken slave."

"We will make it so," said Bat Zor. She had not seen his face in years, nor made love in just as long. Of late, he had preferred the company of Zubaydi concubines and Cathayan courtesans. What was old, wizened Bat Zor compared to a Zubaydi woman, dark-skinned and long-haired, in the flower of her youth—or a Cathayan girl in a silken robe, playing him foreign tunes on the lute? Bat Zor's beauty was long gone. Yet somehow, their spousal bond endured; the King of Kings did not divorce her, nor send her away quietly. He still professed her love for her, even asked her advice. *I love you,* she wanted to say, but dared not, for fear that he would not say the same.

"Leave me," said the King of Kings. "I will speak with you soon."

"Goodbye, Mirzanēs." She dared speak his name. She left safely and quietly, her life preserved despite the disappointing news. She would stay near her husband's cavalcade.

She would watch Eloesus burn.

SWORD AND HELM

There, panting, lay Phillipidēs
Amid the burning desert sun
The amazon had mixed a brew
To cure and mend his grievous wound
But she let him have none of it!
Said she unto Phillipidēs:
"A god requires no medicine
And that is what you are—a god!
So stand up, grab your sword and shield…
No mortal wound can bring you low."

—Arkelaios

COUNCIL OVERLOOK, THEMURIA

Theron's words had stirred the people to revolt. Faced with the angry masses, the kings of Kersepoli—Kyrion and Sardio—as well as the archon of Korthos, Hector, together with Gygax, King of Tharta, had no choice but to make battle plans.

Any hopes of a peaceful resolution and terms of surrender were squandered when the mob cut off the vizier and Bat Zor while they tried to flee. They had dragged the vizier off his horse and stabbed him to death. Bat Zor they had inexplicably left alone.

Yet here the leaders of the Eloesian world stood, on Council Overlook, halfway up Mount Hylea. A circle had been carved into the stone, together with the names of the four cities—Tharta, Thénai, Korthos, Kersepoli—as well as others such as Nautilos whose days of glory were long past. The cliff where the council circle had been carved plummeted many fathoms into the trees below. All of Themuria could be seen from here: the tiny village of Arkadion, nestled amongst the pines; the streams, lakes and ponds which dotted the woods; and even the ominous shape of Devil's Chair many miles away.

Theron gazed into each leader's eyes. Even now, facing a threat, none trusted the other. How could Hector fight alongside Kyrion and Sardio, who just weeks ago had stolen a city from Korthos' control? How could Gygax, the pampered King of Tharta, ever stoop so low as to join forces with this rabble? As Theron pondered, he realized that he did not trust them, either—none of them. Eloesus was too disunited. Their armies, if joined together, would break rank; they would quarrel and fight, even kill each other. *What was I thinking?*

"And so," said Hector, "for the first time in centuries, the cities of Eloesus meet as one. Not since the years of Phillipidēs has this occurred." The silver-haired Archon of Korthos was by far the oldest member of this makeshift council. "Even then, the other cities did not heed Tharta's call. Tharta fought the Megarine War alone, by itself. What makes us think a doom that threatens our very existence will stop our fighting?"

"There is no chance unless we unite," Theron said. *Even then, there is no chance.* "My city has the greatest navy," he continued. "Great enough to perhaps threaten Fharese ships."

"Greatest navy!" laughed Kyrion. "Mankind does not live on the water; only an army will end this war."

Theron ignored the harsh words. "The Kersepolans have the best hoplites in the world… perhaps good enough to face a million Fharese."

"Greatest hoplites," scoffed Hector. "Korthos has a fighting force *double* their size."

More quarreling. Theron sighed. "Korthos has created some wondrous inventions. I saw your colossus. We must put it to use."

Hector frowned. "The colossus is for Korthos and Korthos alone."

"We must stop this!" Theron snapped. Winds were blowing down from the Mount of Prophecy, winds that showed the Oracle's burning disapproval. The winds told Theron, *"Divided, you will fall."* "We have agreed—"

"We have agreed to nothing," Gygax spoke for the first time. Young, wearing a thick robe and a jeweled crown impractical for the weather, his voice oozed arrogance. He had nothing but contempt for these so-called "leaders," little better than country serfs.

"Then we must agree now," said Theron. "Will Kersepoli join the resistance—and fight alongside Korthos, Thénai, and

Tharta?"

"We will," answered Kyrion and Sardio in unison.

"Will Korthos do the same?" said Theron.

"Yes, that is my pledge," said Hector, "and the whole of the Assembly."

"And Tharta?"

Gygax laughed. "No," he answered. "No, Tharta will not."

Theron's heart dropped. His own wife, Zubeida, had cheered along the resistance. Was Zubeida—a southron, a daughter of the King of Kings—somehow more Eloesian than he?

"Tharta will give no aid," said Gygax. "We will remain neutral. The blue cloaks of the Thartan hoplites will not be seen in your army."

Theron could not believe the words. How could it be? "You have betrayed us all," he said, but the condemnation did not seem to faze Gygax.

Instead, he glared. "Fharas is the greatest power in the world. I cannot wait to see how you commonbloods deal with it."

Gygax turned and left, mounting a horse which he had tied to a tree. He left as a wind blew from the Mount of Prophecy, a wind of knowledge, a wind of insight. Despair engulfed Theron like a whirlwind; the strength in his legs gave out a moment but the cold, pure wind steadied him.

As Gygax rode away, Theron looked around at the last leaders of the free Eloesus. Hector's eyes were shallow with fear; there was more dread in Kyrion and Sardio's eyes than either would admit.

"Will you still fight?" said Theron. "For a free Eloesus?"

"Kersepoli will live free," said Kyrion, "or it will die."

"You have Kersepoli's armies, together with its citizens, Elehoi, or slaves," finished Sardio.

"Korthos' commitment will not waver," said Hector. "You have our army, our navy, our colossus."

"Long live Eloesus," said Theron. Together, Eloesus would stand or fall—with one disheartening exception.

THE RUINED TEMPLE, MOUNT HYLEA

After Kyrion and Sardio had left on their horses, after Hector had left in his carriage, when Theron stood alone among the pines and the whispering winds, he returned to a place he had often been.

The collapsed white pillars greeted him and so did the spectral drums which never stopped their pounding beat. Yet there was something different. The grass, poking through the chipped and marred flagstone, was a brighter shade of green than he remembered. The sky seemed somehow more blue. There was loud piping to accompany the drums—and he was not alone.

A satyr with gold-furred legs was skipping around the temple grounds as he played a pipe. Near the temple, a group of satyrs were guzzling bottles of wine—bottles no doubt stolen during the Games, for on them were written the words *"Korthos— Vintage 308"* and *"309."* Other satyrs had gathered around the nude oracle, draped about her as if a garment. The snake twined around her leg was flicking its tongue in annoyance.

It is like olden days, Theron thought, *when the Oracle prophesied with the satyrs and danced to Brecko's pipes.*

"Come closer!" boomed the oracle, and her voice echoed through the clearing. "I will tell you what you need to know!"

Theron approached cautiously. Those white, sightless eyes never failed to unnerve him. Her words often came across as mad babblings; he questioned himself, then, wondering if he was seeking advice from a woman who could not think sanely herself.

The snake scared him, too, with its long, sinuous body, its cold reptilian eyes, its forked tongue. In Eloesian custom, the snake was a symbol of evil, of dark powers, of cruelty, of malice. He stopped a few yards from her body. The satyrs, with their beards and horns, turned to look at him.

"My Oracle," Theron said.

"The first of the dark king's army will arrive soon, Phillipidēs."

Theron would not resist the name anymore. Perhaps, she had worn him down. Perhaps, he at last, was delusional enough to believe it. "Tharta…"

"Tharta!" the Oracle laughed. "Now, and in ancient days, it was the greatest power in Eloesus. Its granaries overflowed with food; its vats were bursting with wine. Ships brought it Fharese silk, and Khazidean spices, and Kheroan silver from afar…

"Yet one day soon, Tharta will be the least of all Eloesian cities. Even its name will be erased. All of its glory will be blotted out. Not in your lifetime, Theron, not in the lifetime of your children or your children's children. But soon."

"What must I do?" said Theron.

"O Phillipidēs," said the Oracle, "You must do much to have a small hope of succeeding. Pyrax and the Helm of Invulnerability must be returned to your godly hands…"

Theron drew Pyrax, and the white blade flashed in the sun.

The Oracle began to laugh. "That is not Pyrax… it is only a replica, fashioned by my handmaids. Nor did you ever possess the Helm."

Theron scoffed. "But I killed the demon—"

"You killed no demon," said the Oracle.

"I destroyed the Mantle of Abraxas—"

"It was your belief that destroyed the Mantle of Abraxas… your surety allowed the blade to cut the demon's blood."

Theron cursed. He threw the false Pyrax to the ground. The false Helm had long been lost. "Where are they?" he asked. "Where can I find the sword and helm?"

"A hero requires no help," said the Oracle. "A hero like Phillipidēs lifts the world on his shoulders, and conquers all."

"I am no Phillipidēs!" Theron cursed. The mountains rolled with thunder. Clouds were blowing in from overhead. The Oracle tossed her snake in the air toward him, and it bit him on the neck. The venom surged through his veins. "I am Phillipidēs!" Theron cried without any doubt left. "Yes, yes, I am Phillipidēs!" He grabbed the false Pyrax, his only sword, and ran back the way he had come, out of the clearing, away from the ruined temple, toward his horse. "I am Phillipidēs!" he cried. "Yes, yes, I am Phillipidēs!"

STAGING GROUNDS, OUTSIDE THE THARTAN PLAIN

The desert let up, revealing grass and wildflowers. As a girl, Bat Zor had loved nothing better than when the deserts bloomed. After a spring rain, blossoms opened up and green shoots appeared; the camels ate well, the dry valleys flowed with fresh blue water. These Eloesians did not realize how blessed they were. They never lacked food or water; their fields and pastures abounded with produce, and what they did not have the merchant ships brought from across the sea. In Shakrath—even as the king's daughter—she had gone hungry more than once.

Those in Fharas thought she was the luckiest woman alive. Perhaps she was. But she still remembered those hard times. Shakrath had been the least of all Fharese kingdoms. Bat Zor's father, the king, had just barely held things together amid an unhappy populace and worryingly powerful generals. In her sadness, when she feared the all-but-certain doom, Bat Zor had gone to the well-watered Fields of Gilgamiel… she had plucked flowers from amongst the green grass. She had uttered prayers to Bel-Nohai but he refused to listen.

These dry grassy plains looked so similar to the Fields of Gilgamiel. She had not been to that sacred place, that place where she hid from her problems, for decades. The dry barrens of Shakrath held sad memories of her former life.

Here, outside Eloesus, slaves were decking war elephants in armor under the instruction of mahouts. Yards away, the hundreds of tiger tamers from Saidoon were relaxing in the hot sun, some rubbing their beasts under the chin, others leaving them be.

Ships were on the way, setting sail from Khazidea, loaded with hundreds of tons of grain. An army of this size ate up entire countrysides; merely feeding all these mouths was an incredible feat, a sign of her husband's greatness.

One tiger tamer, her face painted white, was stretching her legs. She, and all these thousands upon thousands of warriors gathered, had such stern faces. What did they know of fragility and weakness?

Bat Zor the girl had wandered through the Fields of Gilgamiel, idly picking flowers. She had not been as pretty as Bat Zor the Elder or Bat Zor Raven-Eye. In face and form many of her ten sisters outshone her.

Yet Bat Zor the girl, wandering through the Fields of Gilgamiel, despairing at her lot in life, had jumped at the chance to prove herself. A messenger had entered Umron, Shakrath's capital, saying that then-prince Mirzanēs was holding a contest, that whichever woman pleased him the most, he would marry.

Her sisters had scoffed when Bat Zor announced her intentions. But what else could Bat Zor the Forgotten, wandering through the Fields of Gilgamiel, do to improve her life? All her prayers to Bel-Nohai had been spurned. Her offerings to the goat-god Nawäl had been ignored. She would have to risk her pride. She would have to risk everything.

She had presented herself to the young, handsome Mirzanēs—and he had picked her above all.

There had been prettier girls in Shakrath, women with luscious lips and dark lashes and olive skin. Yet Mirzanēs had chosen Bat Zor for her humility, for her "lovely dark eyes" and her "infectious laugh."

Their marriage had endured decades. She had borne him twelve children, even the rebellious Zubeida. Her son Shakur was poised to inherit the throne. Her younger sons served as satraps in far-flung provinces; her daughters were married to kings, even the rebellious Zubeida. She was proud of all of them—even Zubeida in her own way.

Though—when Mirzanēs ascended to kingship—he had removed himself somewhat, he had remained loyal to her even when she grew wizened and old. Who was Bat Zor, in physical form, compared to Zubaydi concubines? They were dark haired and dark eyed, beautiful tigers of the night. Bat Zor was old and turning gray—yet she had remained the chief wife all these years, the apple of the King of Kings' eye.

Surveying the war elephants, the legions of Megiddi horse archers circling through the dry grass and the endless horde of Fharese warriors—five hundred thousand in all—Bat Zor pledged her loyalty to Mirzanēs anew. She would fight for him; she would die for him. Everything in her life she owed Mirzanēs. She would do whatever it took, whatever was in her power, to ensure his plans did not fail. She would see the invasion of Eloesus succeed. She would see Eloesus fall; she would see its cities burn, its temples ransacked, its streets run red with blood.

She would do it for her precious Mirzanēs. She would do it for Bat Zor the despondent girl, wandering the fields of Gilgamiel.

OUTSIDE KERSEPOLI

King Kyrion had chosen five hundred men, the best of the best. They were armed with spear and shield, wearing bronze breastplates and flowing red capes. Their iron helms were decorating with towering horsehair crests. Their wooden shields were broad and rimmed with iron. Such equipment would weigh down any lesser soldier but they—like all Kersepolan hoplites— had carried sword and spear since age seven, when they were taken from their mothers and plunged into the world of battle. They did not fear death, only defeat and shame.

Five hundred hoplites, shield and spear locked together, was all they needed to defend the passage into Korthos, the ancient Valley of Sage. It had seen many battles before. Skeletons were buried in its earth, skeletons of heroes and warriors much greater than Kyrion.

King Kyrion led them away from Kersepoli's gates. Outside, Elehoi plowing the fields stopped to gawk. Kyrion's men cursed at them, shaking their spears and spitting in their direction. The Elehoi had cheered on the war effort, but they were still less than Kersepolan, less than human.

Soon, they would reach the Valley of Sage—and find victory, or death.

THENOA

In the days of riding the lonely stretch of road, Theron's mind raced at the Oracle's words. How was it possible to find Phillipidēs' helmet? How was it possible to find Phillipidēs' sword? The hero had been dead for hundreds of years.

The cold winds of Themuria were long behind him. The satyrs piping in the distance, the nymphs bathing in springs, were a long gone memory. The summer sun beat hot down on the coastlands; the sheep, newly shorn, followed their shepherds across the hills. The grass had turned shades of bright gold, starved for water. Gone were the rains of winter; gone was the beauty of spring. Theron wanted nothing more than to stay inside and drink chilled wine; but he had so much to do. The fate of Eloesus never seemed so grim.

The greatest power in the world was intent on laying waste to its cities; and somehow the Oracle expected the forgotten relics of a hero to change an unavoidable fact—that Eloesus was doomed.

After many days of traveling besides pastures and small villages, the walls of Thénai appeared, proud and tall. The Lion's Gate welcomed Theron home, but he did not feel at home.

Outside the walls, groups of would-be hoplites were training in the heat of the sun. Wearing bronze armor and heaving heavy shields, they ran and leapt and thrust their spears in unison. Thénai did not have a professional army; it was called up from free citizens when the need arose. Yet somehow, they had managed to defend themselves all these hundreds of years. Somehow, in all their wars with Kersepoli and the wild Isteroi, they had managed to keep their liberty.

Inside the walls, amid the noise and smells of the city, the mood had taken a grim turn. Young mothers looked frightened; children noticed their parents' fear, but did not fully comprehend what was wrong.

They faced utter annihilation. How could they possibly fight Fharas? *War is hell.*

Though few men remained in the city—most had now donned the hoplites' shield and helm—there was a small gathering in the market square. Men in chitons discussing matters outside the House of Assembly.

Hyron he recognized, and the old man Nikator. Others he had seen before but did not know their names. They were demiarchs, bickering as always.

When Hyron's eyes met Theron's, his face turned a shade of cherry red. "What a surprise!" howled Hyron. "After all this time, our archon has decided to grace us with his presence."

Hyron could not have been in Thénai more than a day. Tensions were high, of course, and even a small delay by Theron could be taken as utter disrespect. He could not blame him. Yet he would not like what Theron had to say next.

Theron removed his chiton in full view. "The Oracle has spoken. I must resign my position as archon. I must find the relics of Phillipidēs."

Hyron gasped. The blood drained from his face. "Oh help us Amara… we are done for."

"The Oracle is a madwoman," said Nikator. "Half of her pronouncements make no sort of sense. You can't listen to her, Theron. You can't. Please, we need you. Your city needs you… the goddess Amara needs you."

"The gods has already spoken through their servant," Theron said. "The relics of Phillipidēs must be recovered. If they aren't found, Eloesus will fall..."

"Amara help us," Nikator said. "Amara help us all..."

~

Theron had heard the ancient epic of Arkelaios sung many times. He could recall the words even now:

> *He faced his death with firm resolve*
> *Without the Helm invuln'rable*
> *"Now is your end!" the Mad King cried.*
> *Thought he, "my own end lies at hand—*
> *Yet I shall have this small reward."*
> *Then answered brave Phillipidēs,*
> *"This is no end! I will live on.*
> *our name will surely be forgot,*
> *And mine above all glorified...*
> *Achieved, have I, what I long sought*
> *The fame which does not ever fade,*
> *The glory which shall never die."*

He could picture quite clearly Phillipidēs, trapped in the Tower of Stars with the mad king Sosimon, bravely facing his death. According to the epic song, the Megaran beauty Laodikē had tricked Phillipidēs, inviting him into her home for a night of pleasure but secretly mixing poison into his wine. Unconscious, she had removed both Pyrax and the Helm of Invulnerability from his possession.

But after that, where had Pyrax and the Helm gone? The location of Phillipidēs' tomb was long lost.

Theron could scarcely read. Finding a book in one of Thénai's libraries would be extraordinarily difficult. It was times like these that he needed his friend Phaido, goddess rest his soul.

Theron looked up at the High City, easily visible from his vantage point in the market square. He lifted the false Pyrax and shook the blade at Amara's temple. "Why goddess? Why did you take him from me?"

How could he learn? The head librarian might know. Thénai boasted often of its libraries and—in his deliberations with the House of Assembly—he learned of the intentions to increase the number of books and libraries by ten percent each year until— by the year 321—they would have more than Korthos. So much of the Assembly's deliberations were intended to make Thénai's name great, to have bragging rights as the "best in Eloesus." So little had been spent on practical matters—bettering trade, increasing crop yields, maintaining a healthy military. Now, when faced with an invasion by Fharas—the greatest power the world had ever known—they had only gilded statues, brightly-painted temples, and enough books and scrolls to fill a stadium.

~

The chief library lay at the foot of the High City, where the path began winding its way up to the House of the Archon and the Temple of Amara.

Its stone frieze was carved in the shape of amazons and lizard people—the mythical Serpent War which supposedly took place hundreds of years ago. Pillars held up its red-tile roof. It dwarfed the House of the Archon and even the House of the Assembly. Countless hundreds of *talents* had been put into its construction; and many thousands of *doukon* had been spent purchasing rare books from across the sea.

At least, the Thenoans had not stooped to the level of Korthos—openly raiding merchant vessels and taking each book inside, making a copy of each and storing them inside the library. Once, the librarians of Thénai had loaned a book at an exorbitant price to Korthos for the sake of copying—a rare text by an author named Naxaris. It dated back to the forgotten years of the Old Dominion. Korthos had stolen the book outright and refused to give it back; they forfeited their payment. There was no one so dedicated to knowledge as Korthos.

Inside the immense library, the shelves of books were so tall and so close together that Thénai felt cornered. Theron could scarcely read, but he could make out certain terms—a row marked "Geography—Eloesus" and a row marked "Geography—The Far West." One book was marked "The Lands of the Isle Men" on its spine. Another read "From Tharta to Pallistrix—Travels by the Great Laocon."

Other books had words he could not read, though if he put in more effort he could sound them out. Others made no sense— what was "*Otios*" or "*Astromagia*"?

A voice startled him from his concentration. He whipped around to find the librarian standing there in a long robe. He was old, with gray hair and wrinkled skin. His eyes were aloof, arrogant. *What is this commonblood doing here*, he might be thinking. *Shouldn't he be out on the farm, milking his goats?*

"Who are you?" said the librarian.

"I am the Archon of Thénai," said Theron. "Well, I guess that isn't true, anymore."

The sneering expression grew only more potent.

"I need help… the epic by Arkelaios, 'The Thenoan War.' I need to know how it ends… where is Phillipidēs buried? I remember some of the last lines… *Your name will surely be forgot /*

And mine above all glorified / Achieved, have I, what I long sought / The fame which does not ever fade / The glory which shall never die."

The librarian laughed. "Ah, old Arkelaios. He is quite overrated in my opinion. There are much better epics. 'The Song of Fhardush.' 'The King of the Sun.' I always found Arkelaios a bit tired… a bit too delusional. A bit immature."

"I don't care for anyone's opinion about it. I want to know where Phillipidēs is buried. I want to find his tomb."

The librarian shook his head. "Ah, former archon. I cannot help you. No one can help you. That silly old epic does not mention where he is buried… only that his body was carried away, together with his Helm and his sword."

Theron grumbled some curse.

"Many have sought Phillipidēs tomb," said the librarian. "Why would you think you could succeed where so many others have failed?"

"I've had enough of you," said Theron, and walked away.

Where could he find the knowledge he sought? He imagined Amara in her home in the sky—proud, tall, a helmet on her head, a spear in her hand. What would she, the wisest of the gods, tell him?

The midday sun beat hot on the streets of Thénai. Merchants took shelter in their stalls. Most people would be at home—but the men of the city were outside the walls, running and leaping, practicing with shield and sword. Somehow, the Free and Democratic Army of Thénai had to mobilize and put up a resistance. Surely, they would falter against the endless horde of Fharese—professionals all, summoned up from faraway kingdoms. "Help me," Theron prayed. "Help me." But as always, the gods did not answer. No voice spoke from beyond. No helping hand guided his way. And so he cursed, and felt as hopeless as ever.

~

It was late in the day, and the sun's burning heat had begun to wane, when Theron's wanderings took him to a part of town he had never been. The mudbrick shanties and abandoned homes of Bronze Street lay close-by to the sea. The sound of the waves, lapping against the shore, was clearly audible. The people here were dirty, clothed in rags and quite clearly destitute.

One woman sat in the corner, old and forgotten—a widow, perhaps, with no children to help her. Red sores covered her face, and every so often she would swat the flies so eager to gnaw at them. A menagerie of black cats were gathered around her. She was looking at him—with her milky eyes, with pupils as black as the night. He did not see a true human gaze behind them, but something cold and alien, unfeeling. A wooden sign stood next to her: "*Megalia—Necromancer. Ten Thalon.*"

"You want something." Theron shrunk back at the low, gravelly voice. "Megalia can help."

What was a necromancer? "I'm afraid not."

"You seek knowledge," said Megalia. "I can tell you are searching for something. I have all the knowledge of mankind at my fingertips, all knowledge past and present, all lives—great and small—throughout history."

Theron paused. He did not trust the woman one bit. There was madness in her eyes, insanity and bloodthirst. Yet she alone offered to help. "Where is the tomb of Phillipidēs?"

Megalia rose with surprising grace. She laughed thunderously. "The great hero of Tharta. Tell me, in this world, who might know?"

"Phaido," Theron said without thinking. Of all the people in this world, if anyone knew—Phaido would.

"Take me to his grave." Megalia ushered him on.

Theron took the lead, and the black cats followed.

~

Like all graves, Phaido's was outside the city bounds. It was a humble spot underneath a fig tree, marked only with a small stone. His name was etched on it, and Theron's grief returned. He stooped over and ran his finger along the cold stone. "Phaido," he said, "why did you leave us?"

"Back away," said Megalia. "Ten *thalon*."

Theron reached into his coinpurse and fetched the ten silver coins. Megalia slid them into her old coinpurse.

The air turned cold as Megalia stood over the grave. Her raven hair turned the darkest shade of black Theron had ever seen, so black it seemed to suck in all the color around it. Her eyes glowed a fiery purple. Her muscles bulged; sweat covered her body. Clearly, she was in pain.

Terrified, Theron thought of running.

Megalia's voice echoed through the cemetery, louder than any one person could ever shout: "Phaido, come!"

Theron stumbled back as a person appeared, shrouded in white light. Phaido floated above head, clothed in a robe. He was transparent and gossamer-like, tossed about by the wind. "Why have you awoken me?" Phaido cried. "Why have you taken me back?"

"It's me! Theron!" he answered. "I need your help, Phaido!"

"Who is Theron?" the ghost said. "Who is Phaido?"

This ghost was clearly Phaido. Yet he did not remember his

own name—and he did not remember Theron, his greatest friend. "Where is the tomb of Phillipidēs?"

"I do not know! No one in the mortal world knows!" the ghost cried. "If anyone knew, there would be a shrine to worship him…"

"Please help me!" Theron said in desperation, but the ghost was fading, shrinking constantly, disappearing.

"Let me go!" the ghost cried. "Let me go!"

The ghost was now a wisp-like strand of matter; it blinked white and vanished.

The chill dissipated from the air. Megalia was panting and sweating. Calling up Phaido had taken up so much of her energy. *Ten* doukon, *wasted,* Theron thought, *and Phaido does not even remember my name.*

"No one knows, as I said." Megalia used her dirty gown to dab the sweat from her face.

"Then I will have to ask Phillipidēs himself," said Theron.

Megalia laughed. "To go back hundreds of years, nowhere near the tomb… to call up a spirit of great will, to pull him from his place at the Fields of Paradise. Such a feat would take all my energy. I would be wrecked for months."

"I will do anything," Theron said.

"Seventy *talents,*" said Megalia.

Theron laughed. "Not even the House of the Assembly could afford that price."

"Seventy *thalon,*" said Megalia, "and your right hand."

Theron recoiled in horror. "What would you do with a human hand?"

"Do not question my price," said Megalia. "By Nix! I know the herbs to numb the pain somewhat. It will still hurt terribly."

"You are a madwoman!" Theron cried. But what other

option did he have, but to consent? To know Phillipidēs' tomb—to have Phillipidēs' sword and helm—was that not worth more than anything else? What was a right hand, compared to Pyrax and the Helm of Invulnerability? What was a right hand, to wear the armaments of the greatest hero Eloesus had ever known?

Megalia's mad shark's eyes saw his resolve breaking down. "A hand… a hand to have and to hold. A hand to flay, a hand shave to its bones. That is my price!"

"I accept," Theron said, "on my soldier's honor."

"Very well!" Megalia said. From one pocket of her filthy gown she drew out a white crystal. From another, she drew a yellow crystal. Then she began to murmur under her breath.

~

The air took on a deep chill and frost formed over the grass. A wind began to blow, circling around Megalia. There was a faint ghostly voice: "No!"

Megalia screamed. The crystals in her hands blazed like beacons. Her skin grew taut and emaciated. She screamed again—blood-curdling, deafening in its pitch. She fell, but a power held her up, preventing her from hitting her knees.

"Ah!" she cried, "I must tap the Void!"

Swirling circles of black appeared over her head. The crystals in her hands burst into a million scintillating shards, and then were caught up in the whirlwind. Theron took a tentative step back. He thought of running. The whole earth began to shake but panic froze Theron in place.

Megalia's face turned a shade of red. "No! It is not enough! I must quit! I must quit!"

But the power she had begun overwhelmed her. She could not stop her sorcery. She had started something which had taken on a life of its own. She screamed again but she was helpless.

A gash opened up in her arm, pouring blood. A fresh gash burst open her chest, revealing the flesh beneath. A third ripped through her neck. She fell dead but a power held her up.

And a mist was forming, a translucent figure like fog.

Theron saw the face of Phillipidēs. In his death, he was young, handsome, wearing a chiton. In his ethereal state he floated above the ground. "Why have you disturbed me?" he asked. His voice sounded like a multitude. "What is the meaning of this?"

"Phillipidēs!" cried Theron. "Eloesus needs you!"

"Phillipidēs," the ghost said. "Yes, that was my name." Even as he spoke he had begun to diminish; he had begun to fall back into the next realm.

"The Oracle says I am you."

"But you are not me."

"I know," Theron said. "Where are you buried, Phillipidēs? Where is your body?"

"Surely, it is wilted away," said Phillipidēs. "But surely I was buried in Tharta, in the tombs of the kings…"

"No!" cried Theron. "No! You weren't!" If even Phillipidēs did not know where he was buried, there was no hope left, none at all.

"Then Kronos must have taken it… Kronos and his ghouls."

"The trogs?"

"It must be in his mountain home."

Mount Kronos, a great peak, lay far away, near Korthos. It was said to be haunted by demons and skittering shadows—what Theron knew must be troglodytes. Was it there he would find the sacred sword and Helm? He had to try.

"Kronos! Kronos!" the ghost cried as he slipped away.

"Kronos, what have you done with my sword?"

OUTSIDE THARTA

The tall white walls of Tharta stood silent as the armies of the Great King gathered.

Bat Zor could see the archers on the walls, bearing bows and full quivers. They had bronze breastplates over their chests and blue capes, iron helms and blue horsehair crests. The soldiers of Tharta did not resist them, but nor did they give them aid.

An Eloesian guide accompanied the army from the region of Ten Cities, indicating the clearest path to Korthos was the Valley of Sage.

Bat Zor, looking up at the white walls from the road, fumed silently that her own daughter was in there. Tharta did not resist or join the Eloesian armies, but they did not aid Fharas either. She had to change that.

Without warning, she turned and galloped down the road toward the gate.

When she arrived, there was a commotion on the battlements. Archers nocked arrows to bows and waited on a command to shoot. Yet a man shouted, "Halt!" He was wearing a suit of iron mail and his horsehair-crested helm was touched with gold. This was a commander of the regiment. "Who goes there?" he cried.

"Bat Zor!" she shouted back. "The mother of your own queen!"

"None may enter Tharta!" the commander said. "No one at all!"

Bat Zor hated using her powers of persuasion. Throughout her life, she had kept it quiet for fear that the Shakrathites would burn her as a witch. Yet sometimes, desperate situations called for it. She lifted her hands and felt the power fill her, cold and sweet. She directed all of it at the Thartan commander. She whispered her firm suggestion: "Let me in."

"I will let you in!" the commander said. "You are the mother of the queen!"

The gates began to roll open. The city lay open to attack. A crafty woman would call the attention of the army. But she could not; how could she explain Tharta's folly? Her husband, the King of Kings, would learn of her dark powers. She often found him unpredictable, even decades into their marriage; would he have her arrested and tried as a witch?

And so she rode in, the dark rider on a dark horse. She would turn Tharta against its brothers, and then all of Eloesus— even Tharta—would fall in a maelstrom of blood and death.

INSIDE THE ROYAL PALACE, THARTA

Bat Zor remembered these alcoves, this courtyard surrounded by pointed arches. In summer, gardeners ensured the plants did not lack for water, but in this burning heat the bushes had begun to wither.

A group of serving maids were scrubbing the colored tiles. The guards had let her by, but no one greeted her. It was beyond Bat Zor's dignity as the most powerful woman in the world—the chief wife of the King of Kings. As soon as her name was uttered amid the white-paved streets of Tharta, Bat Zor should have been carried high in a litter and a flock of slaves should have attended to her every whim. But alas, in this backward land called Eloesus, the poor called themselves "citizens" and even slaves could take their masters to court.

Bat Zor cleared her throat loudly. The serving maids looked up from their scrubbing. They did not say a word. Angrily, Bat Zor stepped through their washing and dirtied the tiles they had cleaned. It was just as well.

~

Music was playing in the feasting hall, Eloesian music sung and played on a lyre. In Shakrath, priests called music immoral—a distraction from honest work, an unwelcome break in their devotion to the holy gods.

A pair of servants, carrying great piles of white cheese wheels, entered through the door. Another servant pushed a cart crammed with bottles of wine and spirits. Bat Zor cursed again. The servant looked up and shuddered with fright when he met Bat Zor's eyes. Then he hurriedly pushed the cart inside.

In Shakrath, wine was never served. Women never partook and men only had a sip here and there, during religious ceremonies or in the company of foreigners. The high priests had taught that wine was "devil's water," by nature evil. The grape vine was a symbol of wickedness and immorality. When Shakrathites ate their bread, they ate it with water. *Bread and water is all a person needs,* the priests had taught her. Bread, water, and a hard day's work.

Even her husband Mirzanēs, King of Kings, a full blooded Fharese man, did not drink. The Shakrathites considered the Fharese drunkards, but Mirzanēs had heeded his wife's instruction.

Bat Zor felt herself seething. Bad things happened when she was angry. She did and said things she regretted for all time.

Yet still, she took that first step—and then entered the hall of feasting.

~

A roasted pig had been laid out on a spit, its mouth stuffed with nuts, berries and grapes. All around it were loaves of bread, bowls of figs and olives, pans of olive oil, honey cakes covered in frosting, berry-covered pastries, haunches of lamb and greasy beef steaks. The diners came and went as they pleased, filling their plates one-by-one with all these sinful morsels, these sweet-tasting delights which took their minds from hard work, devotion, and the heavenly gods.

The lyrist was singing as he played:

The priestess sought Phillipidēs
"Phillipidēs!" she cried and said,
"What do you seek above all things?
Above all gems and gold and pow'r?"

Then answered brave Phillipidēs,
"I seek one thing above all else:
Fame imperishable and true,
A name exalted for all time."

That Phillipidēs was who these wicked foreigners aspired to. Phillipidēs who—by their own admission—drank wine to excess, who lusted after whores, who sought his own glory and not that of the gods. A nation aspiring to that would surely resemble Eloesus in all its wickedness and filth.

When Bat Zor looked up, upon the dais, where the king and queen were seated, her fury increased a thousandfold.

Her daughter sat there in two-piece clothing: a skirt that went above the knee and a top which stretched tight across her breasts. They were both scarlet, the color of a whore. Her hair was braided in Eloesian fashion and a glass of wine was in her hand.

"There is my daughter!" thundered Bat Zor. "Wily and dressed as a prostitute, a glass of wine in her hand!"

The music of the lyre stopped. The chatter quieted to nothing. Diners looked up, petrified. King Gygax backed away in his seat.

Only Zubeida, her daughter, showed no fear. She glared at her mother, lips perked in a rebellious smirk, chest puffed out tauntingly. She took a sip of her wine.

"So arrogant, so brash!" cried Bat Zor. "Think of the example you are setting for your son…"

"Do not worry about Fharseos…"

Bat Zor gasped. The name was insulting in the extreme. Fharseos was an Eloesian legend, not the true founder of Fharas. They made up stories—invented vile myths to sully the empire. Surely, Zubeida knew how deeply that name would wound her.

"You have no power over me anymore," said Zubeida. "I am pregnant again, mother. If it is a girl, we will name her Eloesa… if a boy, Phillipidēs."

Now, Zubeida was trying to aggravate her, to get under her skin. "Be careful," said Bat Zor. "You do not seem to remember your father is the most powerful man in the world… If I want, I can take you with me. I can turn you into a virgin priestess of Mina…"

"You can't do anything," said Zubeida.

Bat Zor summoned up a bit of her inner power, felt the room and her own self turn cold. She saw that Zubeida was not alone; Gygax's first wife Thelema was there, too, frowning as always. "You are pushing Tharta to war," Bat Zor said calmly. "I cannot take you now. But I will. When this war is settled… you will be taken back to Shakrath. Some of us honor our commitments and our vows."

"Get out!" cried Zubeida, the harlot, the brat. "Get out!"

Bat Zor looked one last time upon the face of Thelema. Then she turned and left.

SAGE VALLEY, THARTICA

At Sage Valley's narrowest point, the five hundred Kersepolans had formed rank two men deep, shields locked together, spears extended.

The iron helm weighed heavy on Kyrion's shoulders. To a civilian it would be unbearable and suffocating in this burning summer heat, but the Kersepolan hoplites were a people set above; and these five hundred, these Chosen, were the best in the world. It is true they had little chance; but here they had their best hope of stopping the Fharese advance. If they died, their stories would be told in the annals of the ages—the five hundred Kersepolan braves and Kyrion, their king.

A shadow began to appear in the mile ahead. As it grew in size and clarity through the summer haze, the deafening sound of untold thousands, marching in unison, became clear. The darkness took shape—an innumerable force approached them. There were countless rows of men—black-bearded, with iron caps, curved sabers and wicker shields, suits of chainmail and iron boots—and far back, the hulking shapes of elephants, weighed down heavily with platforms of archers. Their swaying trunks were painted red and black, in colors meant to frighten. A horn blew, rolling over valley. Though the noise was deafening, and certain death approached, the sage and myrtle bushes did not sway, nor did the wind blow; eerie stillness presided over all.

The front lines stopped their march fifty yards from Kyrion and the army followed suit. Soon, eerie silence joined the eerie stillness. Death was coming; Kyrion could sense it. Even after years of training, death still scared him. Phillipidēs faced his death with bravery, seeking only immortality; but Kyrion was not Phillipidēs.

It quickly became apparent a rider was approaching,

galloping forth on an iron-armored horse. His head was bundled up in a wrapping, in the manner of the desert folk. His dusky brown robe had no ornament or decoration; yet the jeweled saber at his side, and his noble bearing, indicated his prominence.

Close, within spitting range, he halted his horse and dismounted in the same moment. "Where is your leader?"

"We are all brothers," answered Kyrion.

The man, perhaps sensing Kyrion's importance, turned to him and narrowed his eyes. "I bring you word from the King of Kings, the Exalted One, god manifest... the prince of this world and the next. May heaven favor him."

He looked so certain of his safety, Kyrion noted. How easy would it be to call up a javelin and have him slain?

"I am Dabeer, Vizier of Fharas."

He had replaced the old vizier, that Khusruh.

"You have insulted the King of Kings' dignity with your resistance," he said. "Your incredible insolence will not go unpunished. Nevertheless, my king is a merciful god. If you surrender your arms, your armor... if you open the gates to your cities and dismantle their walls... if you fall prostrate before the King of Kings and promise to worship him..."

"Eino! Javelin!" In an instant, Kyrion's fellow hoplite obeyed, hurling from behind.

The javelin pierced Dabeer's chest. Unable to breathe, unable to speak, he staggered backward. His eyes were wide with disbelief at the utter break in protocol. All laws of war had been cast aside, all rules of conduct and dignity—that is how he saw it.

But Kyrion would not entertain insults.

The horse panicked and ran away, still wearing its iron barding. Another horn blew, echoing over the valley and throughout the mountains that surrounded it. Angry jeers were heard from the horde of black-bearded warriors.

They raised their sabers and lifted their wicker shields. Then they charged.

~

The Fharese broke on the shields like water crashing against rock. The Eloesian spears pierced the wicker shields easily; their chainmail was weakly-made. Within minutes of the charge, hundreds of Fharese died and the Kersepolan shield wall held firm. Bodies piled on top of bodies; warriors leapt over the wounded, lying prone with bloody injuries and twitching limbs, only to find deaths of their own.

Before an hour had passed, their once-triumphant charge had faltered; the warriors no longer seemed sure of victory, and the long, hard slog of battle stretched on. The corpses piled on corpses began to form a putrid wall. Kyrion signaled them to advance.

They stepped on the dead bodies amid the groans of the wounded; then, together, they heaved the putrid wall onto the warriors below. The Fharese were spent; pushed back, with little room to maneuver, thousands more died that day, and not a single Kersepolan lost his life.

THE GREAT TENT, SAGE VALLEY

Bat Zor waited in her husband's quarters. He requested her presence when he felt nervous or distressed; he would never admit this.

It was dangerous to be near him; his anger was unpredictable, and even Bat Zor, his wife for decades, did not know which word of hers would inspire a beating. Beneath the godly façade, through the veil which hid his face, underneath his hard exterior, was a quiet soul filled with doubt. He was wise, though not as wise as his father who had vanquished Sur and brought the Elephant Kingdom into the empire. He was strong, but not as strong as people thought.

In Bat Zor's home country, the magi—priests of the fire-god Athra—proclaimed boldly that Mirzanēs was a god in human form, the manifestation of Athra on earth. Yet Bat Zor could tell Mirzanēs did not believe it. He made a great show of it, accepting burnt offerings from peasants. But underneath the outer shell, he was deeply insecure—of himself, and even of his mighty nation, Fharas.

The tent flap rustled. A messenger emerged, his face pallid, his eyes shallow. He was on the verge of panic.

He carried news of the battle; Bat Zor was sure of it. And it was bad news; his fear could mean only that. If Bat Zor wanted, she could penetrate and probe his mind—such was her power. But she only used it in the direst of circumstances.

"The sun is setting," the messenger said. His hand was trembling. "Three thousand of our men have perished. The Jebrashite and Mamrethite regiments have been wiped out."

Mirzanēs' shadowy form could be seen beyond the veil. He

did not stir. "We have used our weakest," he said calmly. "They must be so proud."

Bat Zor might have been surprised at his calmness, but she had taken the unexpected to be normal. Her husband was a man of wild and unpredictable moods. She remembered when he first received news that five hundred Eloesians blocked his passage. He had erupted in wild rage that any would dare resist him. He had cursed and spat. He had ordered the messenger to be drawn and quartered. Thankfully, the messenger escaped with his life.

Yet beneath his calmness—and Bat Zor knew this without use of her witching power—was anger. It was building within him—anger and hate, motivated by fear. If he was humiliated in this war by some act of god, his subjects would rebel: the Surese would throw off their yoke; the men of Rephah would break their ancient binds.

"Tomorrow, they die…" Mirzanēs projected confidence. "We will send in the Faceless."

Bat Zor thought it would never come to that. The best young men from every corner of the empire made up the army's strongest regiment. They had come from the most noble of families, yet had sacrificed their wealth. They had donned the arms and armor of the Faceless and lived and breathed nothing besides war. They were the nation's best.

Bat Zor frowned at the thought, fighting despair—the nation's best, sent to defeat five hundred heathen Eloesians on the battlefield.

SAGE VALLEY, THARTICA

When night fell, the Fharese withdrew.

Kyrion, with his men, walked about the sea of corpses. In the summer's heat they had already begun to stink.

He noticed movement—what he was looking for. A Fharese man was shaking, covered in sweat. A spear had opened his stomach, revealing the blood and innards beneath. Kyrion wondered what his name was. Surely, he had a wife back home, a beautiful Fharese woman who hid her beauty behind a veil.

Kyrion slammed his spear into the man's heart. Then he struck three more times until his breathing stopped. The Fharese man was an enemy; but Kyrion could not help but deliver mercy. All soldiers who fought to a brave end deserved respect.

Vultures were circling overhead. Fireflies lit up the night darkness. The moon was a white crescent, a pale mistress among the stars. For a moment, all was quiet and still. It was now that Kyrion might retreat to a quiet place and offer prayers to the god Tyros, lord of war. But Kyrion was not a religious man. He did not honor the gods like many kings did. When he faced death, he expected no eternal reward. He had come to view the gods as mere figments of imagination—the creations of sad and desperate souls. What allowed him to face death was the knowledge he would be remembered—the only true immortality that could be achieved.

As Kyrion removed his helmet and let his hair free, and set down his spear and shield, a commotion rose above the chirping crickets. Shapes were moving around in the darkness. Eventually, they took shape and form: men in clothes of rough-spun wool, with a mix of spears and javelins, swords and axes. The helmets were mismatched in size, some with horsehair crests and others without ornament. There were hundreds of them, maybe a thousand.

One dropped to his knee. "King Kyrion," he said. "We are citizen-soldiers from Arkadion. We have come to help."

Kyrion laughed under his breath. "Citizen-soldiers," he repeated. "Arkadians all."

The city of Arkadion had pledged itself to Kersepoli. But of all cities in Kersica it was the lowest of the low, beneath contempt and worthy only of scorn. Its people lived rustic lives, with temples built of wood. They suffered long in the snow, but knew little of battle.

"I am afraid you will more hurt than help," Kyrion answered.

The so-called soldier frowned. "You are our king. Will you turn us away when you are trying to help?"

"I want you to leave, all of you," said Kyrion, loud enough for the others to hear. "Let a soldier do soldiers' work. Go back to your flocks and your vineyards…"

"Then we will go to Thénai… perhaps they will not be so ungracious."

"Perhaps not," answered Kyrion. "Philosophers and pederasts. You may do well with them."

The Arkadians turned and began to leave. Their leader lingered. "I have a message from the Oracle… 'For love you will be betrayed.'"

Kyrion did not heed the advice of madwomen. "Leave at once, or I will strike you dead."

~

It was dawn and the battlefield had largely been cleared of bodies. Again, the Kersepolans joined their spears and shields, forming a mobile wall. Ahead, in the Fharese lines, something was stirring. The elephants in the distance were moving away; the army's ranks were shifting. A horn blew, echoing through the valley. Three more peals answered. Soon the front lines began to break away, making way for several thousand stamping feet.

The warriors Kyrion had fought before wore very little armor. The battalion approaching him resembled a wall of gleaming steel. Every bit of their body was covered in iron plates. Over their heads they wore iron masks with tiny eye-slits. Black capes trailed from behind. Each warrior held two curved sabers.

Yet Kyrion was not afraid. He had long put away fear. All panicked concern for his own life was secondary. He reveled in the thrill of battle, the excitement of combat. Even the threat of death itself was welcome; it filled his body with energy and shot power through his veins. It affected him more than a hundred bottles of wine, or a pretty woman's kiss.

A horn blew.

Kyrion and his men had locked their shields and thrust their spears outward. A second row behind had raised their shields above-head and prepared their spears to strike. When the lines held and no enemy flanked them, the phalanx was invincible—an impenetrable wall of shield and spear, a flawless machine meant for killing.

The iron battalion began to shout and then charged suddenly, waving and slashing their sabers in a frenzy. Their momentum was not enough to break the phalanx; again the Fharese broke upon the walls of shields.

The Eloesian spears mostly glanced off the iron-plated armor but a few well-placed blows struck home across the phalanx. Eloesians wore only bronze breastplates, having enough protection from their shields not to worry.

The iron warriors yelled and struck furiously, but slowly the spears began to strike home. A warrior died here and there, pierced through-and-through by a well-placed Eloesian spear. Cries rang out with increasing frequency; yet the Eloesian line did not buckle or break. No Kersepolan faltered.

It was hours into the sunny day before the iron battalion lay dead and injured on the sandy ground.

They had been tested again. Kersepoli prevailed. Against all odds, it seemed to Kyrion that his five hundred Chosen might win the day. The Valley of the Sage might prove to be the graveyard for this monstrous human herd. Perhaps Eloesus would be spared. Perhaps the Fharese would not pass.

With eyes gloomy and disillusioned, the Fharese again withdrew.

THE GREAT TENT, SAGE VALLEY

Bat Zor pitied the messenger as he entered sheepishly.

"The Faceless are slain," he said. "All five-thousand are dead."

Her husband leapt through the veil. He grabbed a candlestick and began a savage beating.

"No!" the King of Kings was crying, "No! My Faceless, my Faceless… bring back my Faceless!"

Bat Zor dared not stir as the beating continued. Instead she shrank back. Blood appeared, spattering the insides of the room. She could not look away. She observed her husband, powerful even in his old age. His crown fell off as he struck the messenger over and over; the bulky object, forged of gold, was studded with diamonds, rubies, and emeralds. His purple robe tore as he hammered the messenger's head into oblivion; it was lined in some places with gold cloth, creating vivid patterns. His beard began to drip with blood; it was white, showing his old age, yet bushy and full.

She had seen the King of Kings. It was said that if a peasant or low-class merchant did the same, he would be stricken dead by the gods. That too, Mirzanēs doubted.

Do not beat him, Bat Zor wanted to say. *He is only a messenger.* But she knew better than to cross him, to question his commands.

At last the messenger stopped his wailing; his body failed to put up resistance. Her husband, undoubtedly ashamed and regretful, dropped the bloodied candlestick. His old hands were shaking. He stood up, face specked with blood. In his old age he had grown more handsome; no longer was he the gangly, plain-faced youth Bat Zor had wed. He had grown larger, fuller, and his white hair and brows seemed to bring out the best in his appearance.

His eyes were full of shame. "Heathens," said Mirzanēs, "Heathen worshippers of a foreign god… they have defeated our best. Morale will collapse, Bat Zor… My warriors will be terrified." He walked over, picked up his crown, and placed it weakly on his head. "I am ashamed, Bat Zor."

Even the King of Kings, god manifest, can be devastated. Bat Zor walked over to him, brushed his cheek gingerly. She straightened his robe, like she had so many times before. She adjusted the crown into its proper position. Then she kissed him. "You have been through much," said Bat Zor. "You have succeeded when you were certain of failure. You crushed the monotheists in Taifun. You beat the magi into submission when they tried to break free of your control. You quashed the rebellion in Rephah. You built the statue of your father in Taifun. Do not underestimate yourself, my husband."

Mirzanēs grabbed her and violently threw her to the floor. "Do not try to comfort me, woman. Comfort is not what I need."

Bat Zor felt her eyes water. She never demanded love of him. His affection was rare. The fact he had not put her away indicated how he felt; how he prized her above all his wives, even when she was old and wrinkled. Yet she could not help but ache at his cruelty. A kind word did not deserve such hatred. He had struck her before, even beaten her, and she never knew when. He was unpredictable.

He retreated back into the veil.

Bat Zor tried to hide her weeping; she sobbed silently, knowing it would only anger him more.

SAGE VALLEY, THARTICA

When the sun began to lower in the sky and the heat became a haze on the horizon, the Fharese made their move. The first sign Kyrion noted was a shifting in the crowd. Beyond the common warriors with their beards and wicker shields, figures began to emerge—great towering figures not human, but feline.

Rows of tigers appeared: great cats the size of horses, some white, some gold—black-striped and white-striped—with teeth the size of sabers. Ropes were tied around their necks and holding the leash were women. Dark-complexioned and dark-haired, their nude bodies were painted in white patterns. It was too bad they had to die.

A civilized nation would not send women on the front lines: women, whose lives should be preserved. It was not for women to die on the field of battle. The other cities of Eloesus claimed Kersepolans were ruled by their women; but they had always been spared this indignity.

"No mercy!" Kyrion shouted through his helmet. "Tyros help them!" A vain plea to a god he did not believe in.

At once the tigers and their female tamers made a go at the Kersepolan lines. The enormous beasts clawed and scratched, but could not pierce the shield wall. One tiger roared as it tried to leap over the shield wall; a spear punctured it through the neck. Its handler began to scream; she drew out knives and, in a wild rage, ran at the shield wall to meet a quick and decisive end.

One woman was seated uncertainly on the back of a sprinting tiger. The tiger, with fur white like snow, vaulted into the air, throwing its rider onto the ground where two spears pierced her. The beast clawed and dragged as it tried to leap over the wall of shields but three spears pierced its furry body and it slid off, smearing shields with blood.

The tiger-less women went mad. Some charged recklessly to a certain death; one slashed her wrists with a knife and fled back into the Fharese multitude.

The sun was setting. The shield wall held. The Fharese withdrew.

THE GREAT TENT, SAGE VALLEY

A man opened the tent flap, startling Bat Zor from her thoughts. He was a eunuch and a dark-complexioned man of Khand. He was part of the King of Kings' entourage, though Bat Zor could not place his name. Was it Hudu, or Rushan?

Immediately the Khand fell prostrate.

"What is it?" said Mirzanēs' from behind the veil.

Still lying face-first, the Khand spoke: "A woman has arrived in the camp. She is begging to speak with you. She is Eloesian. She said she can change the course of the battle. She calls herself Rose Red."

He would have her killed, surely. Of that Bat Zor was certain.

"Rose Red," Mirzanēs' repeated. "That is not a true name."

Mirzanēs did not entertain the company of strange women. He only added them to his harem.

"I will hear her out," said Mirzanēs. "Let her in."

Bat Zor did her best to conceal her surprise. She dared not speak against the decision. The defeats on the battlefield had weakened his spirit; he let his guard down.

Not long after the Khand left, the tent flap opened again.

A woman stood there in a red headscarf and a blue veil. Her red silk shirt had a generous V-cut, revealing much of her breasts. Her pants were so tight Bat Zor could make out the contours of her knees.

And there was something about her presence Bat Zor recognized. She could feel and sense her spirit; they had crossed paths before.

She realized her identity just as Rose Red spoke. "I am Thelema," she said. "I was the wife of Gygax, but he put me away."

Bat Zor could not help but glare at this Thelema, covering her hair yet dressed as a prostitute. No doubt, she had purchased the headscarf and veil in her own city of Tharta, where so many Fharese lived. The Fharese seamstresses there had grown too close to Eloesian culture; they had taken the headscarf, a sign of modesty, and turned it into the garb of a whore.

"It is said the Fharese honor their commitments and vows," said Thelema. "That is better than Eloesian men. I wish to join you. There is a mountain pass which bisects the Valley of Sage… it will allow you to get behind the Kersepolan line and crush them for good."

"We can worry about that in the morning," said Mirzanēs from behind the veil. "Bat Zor, leave us."

"But—" she began. The thought of her husband with this whore…

Thelema removed her headscarf.

"*Leave us!*" boomed Mirzanēs, so forcefully that Bat Zor scurried out of the room.

Tears formed in Bat Zor's eyes as she ran away. At last her knees buckled. Her spirit was fading. *My life is over,* thought Bat Zor. *It is over and done.*

SAGE VALLEY, THARTICA

Before dawn, Kyrion awoke. Like his men he had only slept in shifts, preparing at any moment for a Fharese charge.

Eyes alert, he tied his sandals under the light of the waning moon. The stars were bright and alive, the constellations radiant. There was Fharseos, there the Bull, there the Twins.

He fastened his breastplate of bronze and set the heavy iron helmet on his head. Then, heaving his shield over his left shoulder and his spear over his right, he prepared for battle.

His co-king Sardio would have said a prayer and offered a calf to Tyros. At the minimum, he would have poured a libation of wine over a makeshift altar. Kyrion did not have such faith; in fact, he felt it distracted him. Everything that happened, he had to control; he could not rely on hope and the gods' favor. There was no happy paradise awaiting him, only a coffin and worms.

Yet he had a sense, in this cold morning air, that he would die before the sun set.

He had sensed it before and been proven wrong; but this felt different, as sure as the sun and moon and stars. *I will die today.*

The shield wall had held firm. No single Kersepolan had died, and the Fharese had lost at least ten thousand. The five-hundred Chosen were impregnable. They could not break or bend. *So why am I so certain? I am sure as day.*

The alliance with Korthos and Thénai had been very minimal, in real terms. Sardio did not want to collaborate. To sully himself with those philosophers and boy-lovers was utterly beneath him. Sardio had too much civic pride.

That all changed with Kyrion's certain doom.

Still clad in armor, Kyrion walked down the firm unbroken line. He tapped one hoplites on the shoulder—a valiant fighter of good birth. His name was Pherion.

Pherion turned, his face indistinguishable from the other Kersepolans in the bulky iron helmet; yet Kyrion knew him. "You must ride home," he said. "Tell Sardio to give Korthos the lightning orb…"

Surely Pherion thought Kyrion was mad. What was a lightning orb, Pherion wondered. Why would Sardio want it? "I will live or die with my brothers," said Pherion.

Kyrion had expected as much. "Your brothers at home need you, too."

"I am not afraid to die."

"You served the Chosen honorably. Now a greater task demands your attention. You must obey. Go, Pherion… go, and hurry."

Pherion hesitated, then turned and left the ranks. He walked off to where all the horses were tied and the Chosen's servants kept their quarters. Kyrion took Pherion' place, falling into rank.

~

As the sun rose, the Fharese charged hard, throwing all their energy into breaking the line. Scores of bearded Fharese warriors fell by the Kersepolans' spears. The Chosen continued their advance, stepping over the bodies of the dead and injured. Rains of arrows fell at intervals, but they fell uselessly upon the second row of shields, hoisted above the hoplites' heads.

At midday when the sun burned hot, Kyrion was slick with sweat, and it seemed the very earth groaned for water—the Fharese, exhausted themselves, began to falter. Quicker and quicker, the Kersepolans cut them down, marching in perfect formation as spears thrust out. It seemed they were ready to retreat; then a horn blew from behind.

At once, life returned to the Fharese warriors; they raised their sabers and charged with renewed vigor.

Kyrion spared a look behind, and saw hundreds of riders approaching. The lines would break. *We will die.* "Cut formation!" Kyrion cried. He and the second row of hoplites switched to face the riders.

They rode astride white horses. Their robes were long and deep purple, falling halfway down the horse's height; white turbans were on their heads, and in their hands were staffs like shepherds' crooks. Their free hands they thrust upward; a cold wind blew, and then, fire.

They cast fireballs from their hands, and summoned up great columns of flame. One gout of fire struck Kyrion head on and immediately he began to burn.

He screamed and screamed but none could help him; he had expected an end, but not an end like this.

~

The magi—having crossed the treacherous Pass of Twin Horns to flank the enemy—smiled at the inferno. The five-hundred heathens were utterly decimated. The path was open. Eloesus was theirs.

VICTORY AND DEFEAT

The sun burned bright upon the bier
Where brave Phillipidēs now lay
A life he lost, a gift he gained.
Yea, the fame imperishable!
Yea, the imperishable fame…

—Arkelaios

SUN GOD'S WHARF, THARTA

Demara had lived in Tharta a long time, and had seen many troubles, but never had she been as worried as now. In her youth, she had lived far from these shores, in a land so far away it seemed another world altogether.

Yet if she took a ship and traveled weeks across the tumultuous waters, stopping in ports along the way, on a craft heavy-laden with all her possessions… if she hiked through barren trails across the yellow grass… there, in the land of Dys, the far west, lay cities not unlike Tharta.

Yes, Demara was from the colonies. Thartans had nothing but scorn for the colonies. Yet Demara's home, the great city of Mageios, had shown greater mettle than Tharta ever had. Decades ago, the Fharese Empire had tried to seize the cities of Dys outright. Mageios joined with its sister cities, Lornadion and Agathion, and broke the empire's ranks. Their ships had been dashed upon the rocks; and that was when all her trouble began.

For something more than cargo had washed up on the beach.

"Demara!" she heard his voice, startling her from her thoughts.

Farhad appeared, bearded like all Fharese men. He looked different, now, from when he was just cargo washing to shore. Hints of gray touched his beard and dark hair. Their children had reached adulthood. Yet she had never been so uncertain of their future.

Already, she feared to go outside in Farhad's presence. The hatred and fear of the Fharese was palpable. The Eloesians were careening toward a war they could never win. *How would the inevitable victors treat Farhad,* she thought to herself, peering into his dark yet warm eyes. *He had betrayed his nation to marry an Eloesian.* Should she have spared his life, married him—or should she have sent him on his way? The Fharese did not take kindly to defeated warriors.

The gods had been kind to Demara and Farhad. Perhaps she had angered them; and thus the war began.

Yet she had always been pious, and she was not a traitor. She was an Eloesian to her inmost being. Each year she did her duty; she offered money to the priesthood and made a sacrifice to the civic gods.

She eyed Farhad, who also called himself an Eloesian. In ancient times, a barbarian becoming an Eloesian would have been unthinkable. Only a Thartan belonged to the Thartan family; only a Thartan was a Thartan.

Some now considered Farhad an enemy. She did not. She embraced him as he stood there, and asked the civic gods to protect them all.

THE SHORE OF JOGHEIRA

Kora—amazon, Solarine, grandmother—watched the foreign ships sail by. They were far out to sea in the battering wind and waves: dhows, clearly of southron make.

The morning air was cold. Her mind was filled with a memory—a memory of a time long ago. *No, it was not so long ago. A* man had come to these dangerous shores, a young man in the prime of life. She could not remember his name; yet an air of fortune was about him, and great things were ahead. He had been seeking aid from the amazons, the ancient enemies of man.

Theron. The name seemed whispered in the wind.

The queen Daphnë had refused to help him. Now his very people were in trouble. Could she refuse him now?

A ship was approaching, headed toward Port Ursa. Its three lateen sails were blue and marked with a red four-pointed star. The craft was massive, easily carrying a thousand men. Perhaps these foreigners did not know of the amazons or the dangers they faced here. Here, men were despised. Husbands were to stay at home, never to speak and never to be seen. When these foreigners met the amazons, what would they say and do?

Kora met the sailors as they were docking in Port Ursa. These were surely southrons—bearded men of varied complexions. Some wore turbans and others cotton headwraps. Their ship stank of sweat and grime. On the massive deck of the ship, a hundred warriors idled by, with curved sabers on their hips and shields strapped to their backs.

Kora, as chief advisor to Queen Daphnë, was as qualified as any other to meet them—and hopefully, turn them away without incident.

Soon a man emerged, walking across the plank, followed by the warriors. This man wore a turban with a diamond aigrette. His robes were silken, dyed in purple and scarlet patterns and studded at intervals with blue sapphires. He was dark complexioned, almost as swarthy as the amazons. He carried himself proudly—this was a man of great importance, a powerful lord or overseer of the empire. He glared at Kora. "I, Ahmett, an *emir*, a peer of the empire… am greeted by a *woman*?"

"You will be greeted by women here," answered Kora, sneering. "Here, the natural order is followed… women are the masters of men."

The disgust on Ahmett's face had not lessened; in fact, it grew more intense. "Well," he snarled, "tell your king that the Fharese Empire has a message for him."

Kora already despised this man. "Our *queen* is only bothered by important affairs. A war on the mainland is of no concern to us."

Ahmett swept his saber out of its sheath and in an instant his warriors followed. Rage was written all over Ahmett's face. Glaring, he shouted, "You will pay me proper subservience, or every man, woman and child in this city will be slain."

Kora knew the limits of her power. A flash of flame, a gout of sun-fire, and Ahmett would be burned beyond recognition. Perhaps she could even kill these thousand sailors and warriors. But the seas swarmed with southron ships. The amazons were largely ignorant of the world outside their isles, but they knew the greatest power in the human world lay to the south. Fharas, it was called, the vast lands belonging to the King of Kings. Eloesus was doomed; would Kora also doom the amazons? She could not risk being rude. Ahmett's wrath was dangerous for them all.

Fighting shame, she dropped to her knees. "I will lead you to our queen, Lord Ahmett."

The road wound through the sleepy forests of Jogheira. Once quiet save for the songs of birds, now it was filled with the sounds of five-hundred marching feet. A column of warriors trailed the satrap, marching in formation, bearing shields and sabers. Kora fought sadness as words came to her mind—*it has come to this*. How far her people had fallen. The amazons had once been feared across the world. They had broken the power of the Saurians and slew the Great Serpent. They had repelled all Eloesian invaders—even, long ago, forced the Thartan king to pay tribute.

Since then, their people had dwindled; their great cities shrunk in size. The goddess Amara had forsaken them—that was the only explanation why Kora, an amazon noble, was reduced to bowing before a human man.

At a bend in the road, a black panther appeared on a rock ledge above. It was sleek, as dark as the night between the stars; its eyes were yellow and gleaming. It patted its paws, filled with hatred at the sight of the foreigners. The so-called emir Ahmett screamed and the other warriors drew their sabers.

Kora laughed at their fear. The panther was held sacred by the amazons; so too was the house cat. Sometimes, a surprised panther would attack an amazon; but if she killed one, the sentence was death. To shed panther blood was to become filthy and unclean. If the panther attacked Ahmett—by Amara's will—Kora would watch and do nothing about it.

But the panther only sat there, glaring with its yellow eyes, as the warriors proceeded on.

~

The full heat of midday arrived. The trees seemed to have withered in this deep summer. All standing pools had dried up. A lizard darted by Kora like a fleeting shadow, but prey was scarce.

Every summer, it seemed the world would end; that the sky would never give up its rain, that the rivers would never be replenished. All the creek beds had run dry.

The walls of Tigris appeared, forty feet high and built of giant stone slabs. Within those walls, many deep wells had been dug. Far beneath the surface, water was plentiful. How refreshing it would be to bathe in the icy water. But Kora had nothing to look forward to; only further humiliation and defeat.

Seven archers stood watch over the gate. It had shut soon after the Fharese warriors had been spotted.

"Who goes there?" hollered an archer. Her hair was wild and dark. Amazon bows were renowned for their deadliness; but few humans were strong enough to pull the string.

"It is I, Ahmett, Emir of Bajir!" the grating voice behind Kora shouted.

That voice dripped with arrogance and condescension. Perhaps Ahmett thought the very title of "emir" demanded immediate worship and adulation.

"I come to speak with your... queen... on behalf of the King of Kings' glorious empire!" shouted Ahmett. "I come with five hundred warriors, brave and strong! Open up your gates at once!"

"Lady Kora?" hollered the archer. "You allowed this?"

"Yes!" Kora shouted. *I am sorry,* she wanted to say. *I am so sorry for it all.* "Open the gate! They have peaceful intentions!"

How many more degradations and humiliations could the amazon people endure? How many more before they lost all confidence in themselves, before their very view of themselves was shaken irreparably? *And I play a great part in this.* Perhaps she should have attacked Ahmett... perhaps she should have set their ship ablaze and killed this arrogant "emir" knowing a great war would be started, a war that the amazons would lose.

THE QUEEN'S PALACE, TIGRIS

How grim did the rosebushes and saffron crocuses seem when Kora led a foreign army through them. How grim did the white pillars seem—the pillars of a tomb?

The amazons in the palace did not take up their glaives or their chakrams. Confused but highly aware of their own helplessness, they merely gawked and watched as Kora and the five-hundred foreigners walked by. None fought, none resisted. *What a sad state of affairs the amazons have become*—it was not only her. The only ones who stood their ground were the palace cats. A black cat hissed as they walked by. At last they came to the great doorway which led to the White Tiger Throne.

~

Kora had been to the throne room countless times to offer her advice. She knew its contours and shapes by memory—but every time, without fail, its titanic size and alabaster-white stone took her breath away.

So big, it was, that Queen Daphnë —even wearing her brightly-plumed feather headdress—seemed an ant in comparison. The White Tiger throne was an artifact of another age. No one could create such a masterwork today. It was cut so exactly that it appeared carved out of a mountainside, not constructed in layers. Nor was any mortar used.

Queen Daphnë approached, dark-skinned, with luscious lips and a haughty glare. Clad in just a loin-cloth and a brassiere, no doubt her appearance was shocking to these prudish southrons. Today, she carried a glaive in her hands. "Who is this?"

"This is—" Kora began, but the brash voice of Ahmett overtook her.

"I am Ahmett, Emir of Bajir!" he shouted. "I have come to request—no, *demand*—your aid. The King of Kings has established sovereignty over your islands. We understand you possess a great harbor in Port Ursa and many others on Jogheira. Our ships need winter docking. You will provide them at once!"

Such talk from an Eloesian mainlander would end in blood. If that young man Theron had spoken so rudely, Daphnë would have immediately hurled a chakram or stabbed him mercilessly with the glaive. But she did not react. There was little she could do. "Ahmett," she shouted and began to descend the throne steps. "I have little patience for rudeness. Your King of Kings has no sovereignty over the amazons." Yet her voice was weak; her confidence was gone.

Even in amazon lands, the power of Fharas was understood. None could compete with them. Eloesus was doomed… and if the amazons had lost their ancient war with the Eloesians, then surely they would lose against Fharas too.

"At his name, the earth trembles…" Ahmett drew his saber—an act of incredible rudeness that deserved to be answered.

How badly Kora wanted to kill these men, to burn Ahmett to dust with sunfire.

"Mirzanēs, King of Kings, takes what he wants!" shouted Ahmett. "He is god manifest, and his word is from the heavens!"

"Hail the King of Kings!" shouted the five-hundred in a deafening chant.

"Obey us and you will be spared!" Ahmett shouted. "Do not follow the Eloesians to their dooms. They dared resist the holy King of Kings, and now their cities will be burned… the women and children sold in the bazaars of Bezakirah… the men cut down, or beheaded. Obey us, queen, or every last amazon will be slain, man, woman, and child. Your palace will be a smoking ruin! Your city will be torn down to the last stone!

"All hail the King of Kings! He is god manifest, and his word is from the heavens!"

"Hail the King of Kings!" the five-hundred chanted.

"You may dock in our harbors," answered Daphnë. "We will aid you in any way we can."

Many times, the end of the amazons had been proclaimed. Only this time was Kora certain of it. As she walked home to her house, past the streets, in the waning heat of the day, she uttered a prayer to the Sun Goddess… a funeral prayer. The world of the amazons and everything Kora knew was passing away. Yet she felt in her heart that the transition would not be peaceful—that Kora, Queen Daphnë and all the amazons of Jogheira and the outlying islands were doomed. One way or another, this would end in a maelstrom of blood and death. The amazons' story would end in fire, just as it had begun.

KORTHICA

Theron, bearing a shield, a helmet, and the false Pyrax, had much to fear as he passed along the way. The road had wound along the gleaming walls of Korthos and bent around some low-lying hills. In the distance was a great black mountain, visible through the thick summer heat. Mount Kronos, it was called, named after the demon lord for a reason no one knew. The people of Korthica spoke ill of it, calling it "the Evil Mountain" or "the Dreadmount."

A merchant who had stayed at an inn with Theron several days ago had pleaded to change his mind. "Do not go," he had said. "That mountain is evil."

Yet in that mountain, haunted by trogs, was where the hope of Eloesus lay… the sword and helm of Phillipidēs, the greatest hero of all time. At least, that is what Phillipidēs' own wraith thought—now trapped in the afterlife, floating with the shades along the gloomy river. Somehow that invulnerable Helm and that sword, dipped in Stygian waters, would prevent Eloesus from falling. Somehow it would allow Eloesus to hold fast against that monstrous human herd, sent by a tyrant far away.

Quickening his pace, Theron rode on. So much rested on his shoulders. So much depended on him. He could not help but think he was not up to the task. As far as last hopes went, he was the least dependable.

~

As he rode on, the mountain's dark edges and valleys became more defined. Countless vineyards stretched on in its shadow. Its peak was jagged, not totally black but a very dark shade of ash. He could not help but notice boulders, strewn throughout the land as if by giant's hand—and at the tip of the mountain, a bright red glow.

~

In late afternoon, when he had reached the foot of the mountain, a village appeared—but its homes were abandoned and no villagers walked the streets nor gathered at the well. One man stood there, old and wizened with wild gray hair, with a mad look in his eyes. He was naked but covered himself with a wooden tablet, painted in red splotches. "Turn back!" he howled. "Turn back if you do not believe! The end is nigh! Hail Kronos! Hail Kronos! He is coming with fire and smoke! He will destroy us all!"

~

Theron rode up steep switchbacks, making his way slowly but surely up the mountain. He stopped as there was a great rumble, like thunder, and the earth quivered. A cascade of rocks and pebbles fell from the slope, revealing an opening.

This is madness, Theron thought. But could Phillipidēs be wrong? Surely he would know. Inside the mountain Theron would go… into the deeps beneath the earth where none had gone before.

He tied his horse to one of the scraggly trees that clung to the mountainside. Then, invoking Amara's protection, he entered.

INSIDE MOUNT KRONOS

The further Theron went—the deeper he traveled through rocky tunnels, narrow chutes and sudden drops—the hotter the air grew, the more violent the mountain's shaking.

When it seemed the very world would melt and that the foundations of the mountain would be shaken, Theron fell through a wide hole in the stone—and found himself in a hallway.

This hallway was not natural. It was hollowed out and even carved with twisting motifs. Save for the hole which the mountain's shaking had broken open, the ceiling was arched and carved out smoothly.

Theron's heart shuddered at the thought of this subterranean complex, forgotten by all mankind. He looked ahead—and saw a trog with its wild hair, its leathery skin, its mad eyes. He began jabbering in its own tongue, then turned and fled.

Theron walked forward, feeling no fear. Onward he went—and in the distance, a bright red glow became brighter and brighter.

~

Soon, the hallway became a bridge. Many fathoms below, liquid fire bubbled and boiled. Theron's body was dripping with sweat; his breathing had become strained and labored. He raised his head up and saw the heavens—the blue sky veiled in a thick cloud of smoke. He was in the caldera, in the heart of the mountain.

As the bridge grew narrower and narrower, he walked on. At last, he came to a stone platform, thin and unsteady. There, above the seething fire and flame, was the Oracle.

She stood there, nude, a snake wrapped around her left leg. Her eyes were white and sightless like always.

"Kronos is gone, Phillipidēs," said the Oracle. "You killed his shade on earth. But long ago, he was here—yes, in this mountain he dwelt. As his body began to fail, he had his minions steal your corpse and cast your Helm and sword into the flame. Pyrax lies within this fire, and the holy Helm. But fire cannot overcome them. They remain intact. The sword and Helm, dipped in Stygian waters, cannot be harmed by the hottest of flames. The means of their making was too strong."

"How can I bring them back?" cried Theron.

"Turn around!" boomed the Oracle and in an instant he obeyed.

Hundreds of trogs had gathered, bearing clubs and axes. Some were already making their way down the bridge. All the trogs from the deepest mountain caverns had come to slay him. He could not defeat such a vast number. Not even Zoë could.

When Theron looked back, the Oracle was hovering in the air. The fires below reached their apogee, bursting and flaming, cracking and splashing. Out from the fire two objects were emerging. One, a wingéd helmet of white metal, the other a sword, green in color, made of something like glass. The Oracle drew them from the fire and sent them forth.

When they had come within arm's reach, Theron grasped the sword's hilt and laid the invulnerable Helm on his head. The trogs began to scream. They turned and fled, some falling into the fire as they scrambled.

Theron removed his sheath and threw it, together with the false Pyrax, into the flame.

OUTSIDE KORTHOS

The Free and Democratic Army of Thénai had arrived at last, but they were late.

Ardyo, son of Pythios, had been appointed the Stratego—supreme commander—of the war effort. As the former leader of the Korthian Army, Ardyo had some limited experience in warfare. But Korthos, like all the other city-states, preferred dialogue and diplomacy to war. When a battle happened it was a small affair, not a bloody and ruthless struggle like they faced now.

It appeared the Free and Democratic Army of Thénai was much the same. They were innumerable, stretching far into the distance in a column one-hundred men wide, but their shields and swords were mismatched. These were not professional soldiers; they were blacksmiths and tinkers, farmhands and shepherds.

Korthos and Thénai were so unlike their sister Kersepoli. Yet King Sardio—following the massacre of the five-hundred Chosen—had begun to waiver on his commitments. Perhaps it had dawned on him that their mission was foolish, that resisting the Fharese Empire was futile.

Ardyo still thought the same. But the people had spoken; they would resist. They would fight for their homes, for their families, for their democracy and their right to vote in the people's assemblies. For them, death was better than living under the rule of the Fharese king: better the grave than slavery.

Messengers had already reached him, that the Fharese Army had begun pouring through the Valley of the Sage. They were just days away from Korthos. Ardyo had never been more sure of their ultimate doom. If the five-hundred Chosen could not stop them, how much more would the Free and Democratic Armies of Thénai and Korthos falter?

It was late in the day when the earth shook underneath Ardyo's feet. He turned, and in the distance, he thought he saw a red glow amid the haze. The soldiers of the Free and Democratic Army paused from their drills to turn and look. What had happened? Surely, the hierophants would call it an omen—an omen of bad fortune. Yet Ardyo did not need any sign from heaven to be certain of their ultimate doom.

As dusk fell a large group of men approached, many hundreds in size. Some hoplites gasped and drew spear and shield; but it became clear these were no Fharese. They were Eloesians, clean-shaven, short-haired, bearing mismatched swords, shields and bucklers. When one spoke, Ardyo knew they were Arkadians: "The five-hundred Chosen rejected us," said the leader. "Are you the Ardyo we have heard about?"

What would happen, Ardyo wondered, if a group of rustics from the Fharese countryside approached the King of Kings? Surely he would answer harshly. Arkadians were the most mocked of all Eloesians; they were the butts of jokes in taverns from Tharta to Thénai. Yet Ardyo did not scorn them. Any help was needed. "I am Ardyo," he said. "You are welcome to fight."

"Thank you, Stratego," he said. "Me and my Twelve-Hundred Arkadians will fight to the bitter end. I have brought you a gift…"

"A gift?" Ardyo said. Perhaps he had already ceded too much by speaking to this Arkadian. The Arkadians, wild and ignorant—knowing more about the love of goats than the love of women. There were so many mocking songs about them, so many jokes hovering at the tip of Ardyo's tongue.

The Arkadian leader reached into one of the pockets of his tunic. He brought out two objects—a wilted flower, and a small patch of lambskin. "These are both from the Oracle."

He took the patch of lambskin and saw words written upon

it: "*Look to the mountains for your help.*" More mad words from a mad woman. Ardyo laughed lightly and shoved the writing in his pocket. "And what is this?" he said.

"A hyacinth," said the Arkadian. "I don't know what it means."

Ardyo's stomach twisted at the thought. He took the wilted, shriveled blossom. His wife had been dead many years, but he still could not forget her, nor did he stop expecting to see her when he awoke in bed. Everyone on Tanners Street, where he lived, thought her mad; she spoke ceaselessly of her visions. A melancholy outlook and a deep sadness had followed her all her days; yet she spoke of her happiness in the springtime, "when the hyacinths bloom." Every time he saw the hyacinths blooming, Ardyo thought of her. *Sweet Mykalë, rest in Paradise forever.*

He held the wilted hyacinth blossom to his heart. Then, as the Arkadians walked away, he placed it in his pocket, swearing never to forget Mykalë nor her happiness in the springtime, when the hyacinths bloom.

~

In the light of day, Ardyo's field marshals made a count of the hoplites under their command.

Armed with this knowledge, Ardyo took his army—twenty thousand Korthians and ten thousand from the Korthian allies, thirty-thousand Thenoans and five-thousand Thenoan allies, together with the twelve-hundred Arkadians—more than sixty-five thousand hoplites in total, to face certain doom, to face an army far better prepared. The Fharese would slaughter them, surely, but Ardyo would remember Mykalë in the Fields of Paradise, and how happy she was in the springtime, when the hyacinths bloom.

KORTHICA-THARTICA BORDER

Bat Zor, cast aside by the husband she had loved, fought a battle simply to function. *Cast aside*—her thoughts were racing—*for that whore, that Eloesian woman Thelema, who betrayed her husband and her nation.* She rode on, the Rider in Black, following the army—but the black she wore felt like funeral garb. She was mourning a lost life, a vision of herself which had died, a vision of love and marriage which had been swept away with the wind. Her heart was no longer with these warriors nor with her husband. She was lost.

She felt now as she had, when she was a girl, a Shakrathite, a young daughter of a poor king in an impoverished kingdom. Yet it was worse now; she did not have the Fields of Gilgamiel to comfort her—she did not have those bright flowers or those deep springs. There was nothing she had, just sorrow. The grief, hanging over her like the Messenger of Death, weighed so heavily upon her that she fought just to stay on the saddle. No war could compare to the struggle of just continuing on; and all her prayers to Bel-Nohai did not comfort her—instead, they just made it clearer than ever that the gods were far from her. There was no hope left. Now she was old and cast aside; her daughter despised her. Nothing lay ahead for her except for death.

Her powers over others still remained in her grasp. Could she risk influencing the mind of her husband? Could she poison him against the whore Thelema?

Yet even if somehow she succeeded in that endeavor, she would not be happy. That love would be unearned; it would not come from Mirzanēs' heart. His "I love you" would be shallow and meaningless. His "I am sorry" would have no significance.

As she rode on like a mourner in a funeral procession, she

eyed the yellow hills and thought of running away. Perhaps she could flee altogether from her thoughts. She could flee from her husband's betrayal; she could flee from her feelings. She could flee from herself.

What a terrible difference a week could make. A day, an hour, a minute—such a small instance in time could ruin one's life forever. A dark shadow would haunt Bat Zor's life the rest of her days.

~

At night, they stopped and the army's slaves began setting up tents. Warriors started fires with brush and bundled twigs, then took out their cookpots. Food was running low. All these thousands upon thousands of warriors were impossible to feed. Messengers had assured them a new shipment was coming. For now they had to subsist on dried beans and small rations of grains. But a fleet of ships—many hundreds of dhows—had traveled from the rich breadbasket of Khazidea, bringing enough food to sustain them for a week. More fleets were coming and the peasants of Khazidea surely suffered for it; all the food they had grown and all the food they had stored in their granaries—everything that remained—was sacrificed for the army. All this—for her.

Yes, for her. This invasion had not been Mirzanēs' idea. Although he now supported the effort more than anyone, it was Bat Zor who had started it.

"Look at those haughty men," she had said of the Eloesian diplomats. They had come from Thénai to negotiate terms of trade. Before the King of Kings' many-stepped throne, they had refused to bow and fall prostrate. *We are not slaves,* they had said, *nor are we subjects.* They did not acknowledge the King of Kings' godhood nor his dominance over world affairs.

As they walked away, in the baking midday sun, Bat Zor's heart had been filled with wild rage. She wanted nothing more than to see their blood spilled, to see their arrogance and pride replaced with fear and panic. She had wanted to wring their necks, to beat their heads against the sharp stone steps. Yet Mirzanēs, sensing her anger, had laid a hand on her shoulder. "Calm yourself," he had whispered, but his normally soothing voice had failed to quiet the rage.

She had spoken later on to scholars with vast knowledge of world affairs. She had learned the cause of these diplomats' great arrogance; she had learned that in their barbaric land, the people—serf, peasant, and rich man alike—cast votes in favor of this or that law. They had no respect for nobility or bloodline; they had no regard for the natural order. Thus each man and woman—wealthy and poor—viewed themselves highly. They bowed to no one—not even the King of Kings himself, God Manifest, *padisha*, the greatest power on earth.

For weeks, she had tried to convince him. "Humiliate them once and for all!" she had cried one night. "Make slaves of all of them, these arrogant 'democrats!'"

But it was Mirzanēs that had to convince himself. It was not until he learned that Eloesus—far from being a forgotten backwater—had great wealth, gleaming cities, and a teeming population, that he decided to invade. "It will not be a notch in our belt," he had said to her, "it will be a jewel on the crown of the empire."

It had taken years to plan, and months for the petty kings, emirs, and pashas to respond—one by one—in the affirmative. It had taken many more months for the vast army to coalesce. So much planning had gone into this. Nämer, Great King of Khazidea, had agreed—despite his wishes otherwise—to provide the grain and the fleets of ships. And then, after all this monumental effort, the troops had left the glittering streets of Seshán.

At some point, when Bat Zor had arrived in Tharta and the palace of King Gygax, her heart had wavered. She had seen the people for what they were—good and hard-working, not proud and haughty like she thought. She had seen a people glad-hearted and joyous; compared to them, Fharas was all gloom and despair. She had seen their festivals, their brightly-colored temples, and how the wine they drank so freely seemed to lift their spirits. She had wavered; she had tried to warn the Thartans of their coming doom.

But then she had realized that—even with all the knowledge in the world—the Thartans could not possibly stop the onslaught. She had tried to work up her ancient rage; to despise them and hate them and yearn for their destruction. She had failed.

"My queen," a voice interrupted her thoughts. He spoke Eloesian. Perhaps, this was one of the Eloesian mercenaries accompanying the army. The Ten Cities had pledged five-thousand men for coin—how quickly these eastrons turned on their own.

Bat Zor hopped off the saddle. This Eloesian did not pay her due deference. His voice did not tremble; his knees did not bow. She smiled. It was typical of his kind. So arrogant, so proud, respecting neither kings nor queens.

One hand on her horse's back, she moved up to this Eloesian. In the dim light, she made out a head of curly brown hair, a handsome aquiline nose, a small moonlight gleam in his brown eyes. In his hands he carried a giant wicker basket. "What is your name, Eloesian?"

"My name is not important," he answered. He was a wearing rough-spun brown tunic and a pair of tattered pants. He looked like he had traveled long and far. This was no mercenary from Ten Cities, nor an auxiliary from Tharta. This was an Eloesian—a citizen, they were called. He did not work in the employ of her husband the King of Kings.

"What are your intentions?" she asked him. "Why are you carrying that basket?"

"I have two gifts," said the man. His accent differed greatly from Thartans and Korthians. "Both were sent by the Woman on the Mountain, Her Majesty, sacred Io. All gifts come from the holy Mount of Prophecy."

Bat Zor reached for the basket, but the man jerked out of her way.

"The first gift is a warning," said the man. "Sacred Io does not know all things, whether success or failure lies ahead of you… But she did see you in a dream. She said 'Beware your ships; do not take shelter.'

"And this gift," the man said. "Sacred Io cautions you: do not be afraid."

When Bat Zor took the wicker basket in her hands, she was surprised at its heaviness. The man turned and left, disappearing into the night. She opened the lid of the basket, and there—to her astonishment—was a snake. Instinctively, she dropped the basket, though—strangely—she felt no fear. She did not scream or run. Instead, she stood motionless and calm.

The snake was immense, with a body as thick as a log. As it left the safety of the basket and raised its head, Bat Zor peered into its eyes. Those eyes were yellow, cold and cruel—perhaps evil—like every snake, but behind its icy gaze Bat Zor sensed an intelligence and wisdom beyond her own. So great was the wisdom behind those eyes that Bat Zor thought it might know everything, past and present.

As it slithered up to her and twined around her leg, Bat Zor did not flinch or resist. She did not think it would bite her or constrict her. She trusted this snake more than her husband the King of Kings; more than her children—even more than herself.

Underneath her black robe—her *thawab*—it wound its way

against the bare skin of her leg. Goose-prickles appeared all over her skin as the snake wound its way between her legs, then around her chest; and tightened. She cried out in ecstasy. It had been so long since she and her husband the King of Kings had made love but for now, she felt like a girl again, a humble Shakrathite maiden on her wedding night.

The snake emerged through her collar, through the opening in her *thawab*. Its yellow eyes peered at her, closer than before. It flit out its forked tongue. Only looking into those eyes at such close proximity did she understand the gift; this snake had been sent to aid her in the way she really wanted. This snake had come to kill Thelema.

KORTHICA-THARTICA BORDER

Ardyo, son of Pythios, had set out his army into position along the Royal Thartan Road. Once this wide highway would have been choked with merchant caravans, pilgrims and travelers from all over the world. Now it lay empty and silent—ominously so. The Fharese army lay less than a mile away. And Ardyo had no hopes of beating them; yet he tried not to let it show. These, the Free and Democratic armies of Korthos and Thénai, needed sufficient morale just not to break up and run. When faced with death, the natural response is to flee; only soldiers were trained to run into danger. And these were no soldiers. They were potters and tanners, shoemakers and coopers, farmers, goatherds and shepherds.

And the signs from the gods had been equally ominous. A messenger had run up to Ardyo the prior day.

"Mount Kronos has burst into flame!" he had said. "The countryside is buried in pumice stones!"

A hierophant had explained the omen: "The gods do not favor our mission. They think we are proud to resist the King of Kings. They scorn our arrogance…"

Yet the neither the hierophant nor his associates had abandoned the army; their powers of thunder and lightning would remain at Ardyo's fingertips. The hierophants had told no one else of their dread pronouncement. Still, the Free and Democratic Army had hearts full of false hope.

Ardyo—standing at the head of the army—turned to look at what he had created. The so-called soldiers had drawn their spears. They had formed a wall of shields stretching almost a mile in length. He could not help but feel a stab of guilt. He was somehow responsible for their deaths. They had agreed enthusiastically to fight, to defend their cities and greater Eloesus itself.

Yet when their deaths inevitably followed, was it not Ardyo's responsibility? Was it not him who had led them here, to the place of their massacre?

A great horn blew, loud and blaring. Three more followed, then a dozen. The distant sound of many thousands of marching feet began to echo across the plain. Five hundred thousand Fharese warriors awaited them. The Eloesians would be slaughtered; but how quickly?

Ardyo was not a religious man but he began babbling prayers under his breath. His hands grew clammy and his grip on his spear slipped. "Steady!" he cried. "Today we fight not for Eloesus, but for all mankind…"

OUTSIDE KERSEPOLI

For Pherion—the last of the five-hundred Chosen, the one whom Kyrion had sent forth—the road had not been kind. The journey, stretching hundreds of miles, had gone on ten days in the brutal summer heat. His legs and back were sore from riding. He stank from days of sweat and grime, so pungently he himself could smell it; and his stomach, having fed on dry road-bread and water, for all those days, was in desperate need of true food.

The walls of Kersepoli—when they appeared—never failed to take his breath away. Far taller than those of the other cities, they seemed to stretch to the very heavens themselves. Along its walls, immense reliefs of Saurians, tentacled monsters and skulls could be seen even from Pherion's vantage point. These walls could never falter. They could never fail. All Fharas, in its untold millions, could not break them. Where the rest of Eloesus might burn, Kersepoli would remain.

The streets of Kersepoli were wide and ambling. And now, they felt different. As Pherion rode through down the main thoroughfare, he could not help but notice the tense mood which had fallen over his beloved city.

A woman, beautiful and black-haired, stood on a street corner with a pail of water in her hand. She was glaring at another woman across the way, who matched the gaze in hatred. Kersepoli was always noisy; its women, notoriously loud and opinionated, loved nothing more than a quarrel.

And most strangely, there were men here, and not just slaves and Elehoi. Free adult Kersepolan males, wearing scarlet capes and shields and spears on their backs. In the midst of a war they were at home, as if in a time of peace. Had they truly backed out of the war effort? It could not be.

At the foot of the High City—where the white-pillared temple of Tyros towered over the streets—the palace lay, quiet and undisturbed, protected by a cadre of scarlet-caped hoplites.

"Hail Pherion!" one said.

Pherion nodded. "I must speak to the king…"

As one of the five-hundred Chosen, his right to speak with the king as an equal was unquestioned. Pherion dismounted and tied his horse to a post. The cadre of hoplites stepped aside.

~

King Sardio, seated on the throne, frowned as Pherion entered the room.

Pherion removed his helmet and knelt before him.

Sardio's throne—like Kyrion's right next to it—did not have the immense size or ornate decorations of the Thartan throne. Like Sardio himself—wearing a gold laurel wreath on his head but no purple robe or jeweled rings—the Kersepolan palace was plainly decorated.

"Speak," said Sardio.

"Your Majesty," said Pherion, "King Kyrion is dead."

"As expected," Sardio answered.

His words were callous, perhaps a bit cruel, if not true. Who could imagine a force of five-hundred Chosen holding off Fharas—the greatest power the world had ever seen? Kyrion had always thought highly of his Chosen, but perhaps his supreme confidence was undeserved.

"And the war effort—" said Pherion.

"The war effort?" said Sardio. "The so-called 'Stratego of

the Democratic Armies' came here, expecting me to risk all our lives on this foolish quest. I had gone along with it, but Kyrion is dead—and common sense will prevail. We will make peace with Fharas. We will surrender."

"I cannot think of a better way to spite Kyrion," said Pherion, "a better way to curse his memory, to spit on his grave…"

"The boldness of the Lions will have us all killed. The Pigs know when a war is lost…"

Pherion cursed under his breath. Over the years, two factions had developed in Kersepoli, two modes of thought which had turned into core identities.

The Lions believed in constant expansion, in taking cities from Thénai and Korthos and Tharta—in seizing new land. They believed that the Elehoi were worthless, not even people—and that slaves were "talking tools."

The Pigs believed in surrendering the stolen cities; in freeing the Elehoi and the slaves. Just months ago, when the Kersepolans had seized the city of Bactris, the Pigs—outraged beyond compare—had rioted in the city square. Covered in fake blood, they had demanded King Kyrion pay for his crimes. They had screamed for the execution of King Kyrion; even called for the murder of soldiers. The mob had tried to storm the High City and deface the temple of Tyros, but had been driven back.

Sardio had claimed to be impartial, sympathizing with neither the Lions nor the Pigs. Yet his sympathies with the Pigs were always suspected. Now there was no doubt.

Most Kersepolans had come to identify with one faction; for some, it became the core of who they were as people. There was no Kersepolan anymore—there were only Lions and Pigs, full of hatred for each other, ready to break into violence at a moment's notice.

Pherion had long considered himself a Lion. Kersepoli had

become the strongest military power in Eloesus; and these Pigs wished to throw it all away. They cried for the blood of soldiers even as their hearts ached for the enemy. There was only one thing Pherion could do—one thing, as a proud Kersepolan, as a loyal citizen of his city.

In a single motion he stood up and drew his spear from his back. Then he hurled it hard, impaling Sardio straight through. Sardio gasped and stumbled back in terror.

The royal guards drew spears of their own and Pherion yanked his sword from its sheath. From a strap on his back he heaved his shield forward. The guards came at him; one slashed but overstepped; Pherion dashed forth and plunged the steel blade through his chest.

He had committed the most heinous offense—the murder of a king and the murder of a brother-in-arms. He had, no doubt, started an intra-city war—and he had no regrets.

ROYAL PALACE, KERSEPOLI

As alarm bells sounded throughout the city, and open bloodshed consumed the streets—Lion versus Pig, warrior versus pacifist, brave man versus coward—Pherion, sword still wet with blood, looked on from the palace balcony. Near the market, a fire had been started. That was a true Pig tactic; they generally avoided open conflict, but instead set garrisons or government offices on fire, then ran away.

The words of King Kyrion, the last brave king, echoed through his mind.

"You must ride home," he had said just hours before his death. *"Tell Sardio to give Korthos the lightning orb…"*

But what did he mean, and what was the lightning orb? He had heard faint rumors of this lightning orb—an ingenious invention whose method of making had been lost: a masterwork of brass gears and wheels which produced—in the right conditions— a bright and blazing flash of lightning. Yet where could he find it?

Pherion had slain four royal guards. His sword was lathered in bright red blood; his spear had broken when he tried to yank it from King Sardio's body. He was a wanted man, a criminal—and the theft of the lightning orb was nothing compared to regicide.

From the balcony, if he looked upwards, he could see the towering High City, and the edge of the great temple of Tyros. Tyros, god of war, did not care for Kersepoli more than he cared for Thénai or Korthos. Though the god of war, he was—for all wars—neutral. Yet perhaps he loved Eloesus, the country that— above all—revered him. How many white bulls had been sacrificed to him, how many cows and goats and sheep? Surely he would help his city against the heathen Fharese.

Help me, he prayed, mouthing the words, but no lightning came down, no arrow of insight. There was no revelation sent, like Tyros had given to the heroes of old. Who was Pherion to ask for the help of heaven? He was one of the five-hundred Chosen, a great hoplite among great hoplites, but compared to Tyros and the heavenly beings he was as low as dirt.

~

Instead of revelation, Pherion resorted to hard work. The sound of fighting was audible from the palace's dark and twisting corridors, but Pherion ignored his own fears and worries, his own quickly-beating heart. He had begun something terrible, a chain of events that would surely end in a massacre. Perhaps Kersepoli would no longer be a power anymore. Perhaps the city would fall. It did not matter. Pherion had a command from the true king—Kyrion the brave, Kyrion the Lion, Kyrion the strong. Perhaps Kyrion would not approve of the murder of Sardio—but even Kyrion was wrong sometimes.

Eventually, he found himself back in the throne. How simple it looked, how ordinary. The throne in Tharta was a massive edifice, built to impress. These two plain chairs were meant to emphasize a hatred for luxury—and an acknowledgement that the kings, far from being set above, were hoplites, expected to fight at the front of the battle. Sardio had failed in many ways, but above all in forsaking his role as a hoplite. He had been a Pig through and through.

Where in Varda could this supposed "lightning orb" be? Behind the two thrones, the room—beyond the reach of the wall sconces—fell away into shadow.

Pherion yanked a torch free from the sconce and entered the darkness.

In the oily heat and light of the torch, Pherion peered through rows and rows of shelves. These shelves were crammed with scrolls, marked with tags along their edges. One read "Tax Documents—Fishmongers Street, Year 309, Summer Quarter." Another read "Marriages—Temple Ward, Year 305." A film of dust had collected on these scrolls. Apparently they were little used and forgotten. Neither Kyrion nor Sardio were men of learning. Like most Kersepolan men, the art of letters and reading was—at best—an unimportant subject in schooling. Education was done in the camps, involving extreme physical toil, strength training, javelin-throwing and swordplay; history, mathematics and reading were often not covered at all. Their society did not value men of knowledge, only men who could hold the line, shoulder to shoulder, in a phalanx.

He continued on, seeing the roof far above open up into a towering barrel vault. The shelves stretched halfway up the ceiling, built of rickety wood, crammed top to bottom with scrolls.

"Hey! There he is!" a voice shouted from behind, where the thrones lay. The sound of metal boots echoed through the dark. He counted a dozen men—far more than he could handle.

He took off at a sprint.

The room ended abruptly. A wooden desk lay there at the end, displaying curiosities—an archaic bronze helmet from a prior era, a bronze sword, a few dozen warheads. A large brass ball was perched precariously on the surface, threatening to roll over.

Pherion turned and readied his sword, dropping the torch on the ground. A dozen dark shapes were hurrying toward him. *This is the end,* he thought. *My death awaits me.*

A scroll burst into flames, followed by another. The torch had rolled away from him, toward the shelves.

"You're dead, Pherion!"

Pherion recognized the voice from somewhere but could

not place a name. These people intent on killing him had been his brothers-in-arms, his neighbors, his friends, his fellow Kersepolans. *What have I done?* Pherion asked himself and wondered, for the first time, whether he had made a terrible mistake. The Lions and the Pigs despised each other; but were they not all Kersepolans?

As the heat blazed, growing more intense by the moment, Pherion fumbled and staggered back. The brass ball hit the floor. For a reason he did not know, he picked it up and saw strange runes written all along its sides. A large brass button covered its top, marked with a lightning bolt. It struck him, then, that this was the sacred lightning orb, which he had scoured all of the palace to find. Without thinking, he pressed the button and felt the lightning orb become weightless. He stepped back as it floated there, levitating all by itself. The brass shell slid away and crackling, sizzling lightning spat sparks into room. Fire and lightning combined and the room blazed with energy. One firebolt went sizzling toward Pherion's would-be killers. They screamed, turned and ran.

Pherion grabbed the spitting, sparking orb and pressed the button again. The lightning winked out and the brass shell slid into place. Pherion hid the priceless wonder in the crook of his arm and took off at a sprint. He would sprint all the way to Korthos if he had to.

KRONION HILL

In the dark of night, when the stars were spread like a mantle across the sky, when the moon glowed white and full, when the nightingales sang their eerie melody—Bat Zor watched the food arrive. An endless caravan—heavy laden with sacks of flour and pots of oil and bags of salted meats—stretched into the distance, far beyond the camp. They had come from the west, from Tharta where they feared no incursion. The food would feed these hundreds of thousands for a week. Already a shipment of equal proportions was being sailed from Khazidea. The Khazidean peasants would surely starve this summer; all the fruits of their toil would go to the King of Kings Mirzanēs.

Bat Zor could see well from her vantage point. She had left the massive Fharese camp—larger than a hundred cities combined—and found sanctuary on a hill.

This hill had spoken to her, inviting her to come close. It stretched high above the flat plains surrounding it. No doubt, this hill had been crafted by mankind. Along the crown of the hill, Bat Zor had discovered stone foundations and a sunken plinth without a statue. Writings in a strange language—neither Eloesian nor Fharese—were etched on a small stone tablet, which itself had been broken in half.

Bat Zor, who alone out of the King of Kings' harem had been educated, had begun to develop a theory: this was unhallowed ground.

The old gods had been worshipped here, gods of forked tongues and twisted horns, gods with the heads of animals and the claws of reptiles. In the days of ignorance, human sacrifice was performed; in ancient Shakrath, even the flesh of the victims was consumed. The old gods were called demons, now. Priests throughout the world condemned them utterly; every king and every queen of every kingdom had their worshipped outlawed. It did not seem long ago, those days when children were slain to sate the old gods' bloodlust. It did not seem long ago, those days when war captives were burnt alive to please Lothan or Baa'oul.

She grabbed the tablet from its place, half-buried in the dirt. The writing was inscrutable. Its words were indecipherable. No nation used these letters anymore.

Yet Bat Zor could feel a connection, stretching back hundreds of years, to the carver of these words. Her imprint was faint, this dark worshipper. Her name was far beyond Bat Zor's reach. She had lived before there was any concept of "Eloesus" as a nation.

She had lived when the worshippers of the new gods had grown intolerant. Yes, Bat Zor could sense her anger and her hate—the priests, whom this woman despised, had sentenced her fellow "old believers" to death. Even now, the imprint of this woman's hatred remained. She had been here before, offering human lives before her dark lord.

She relived the memory of this woman—her name was Mallistrix—as she carved the words into the stone.

And then Bat Zor—feeling this woman's pain and hearing this woman's thoughts—read the tablet in full.

TO KRONOS OF THE MOUNTAIN, WE BEG FOR YOUR AID. CRUSH THE THARTANS AND ESPECIALLY PHILLIPIDĒS. KILL PHILLIPIDĒS THE ARROGANT, THE WICKED. KILL PHILLIPIDĒS THE SON OF THE PRIEST.

The rest of the tablet had been broken off, yet Bat Zor, sensing this woman's intent, dropped the jagged stone and read on.

TO KRONOS, O! THE SCREAMER IN THE

MOUNTAINS WHO SENDS THE PEOPLE MAD! KILL
PHILLIPIDĒS THE PROUD, THE ARROGANT! LET
SOSIMON DESTROY HIM...

Bat Zor had heard enough of these Eloesians' foolish legends to know this Mallistrix had been disappointed. According to the songs the Eloesians sang, Phillipidēs, the companion of prostitutes, the drinker of wine—that is, devil's water—the proud and boastful, had succeeded. He had died in battle "as he always wished" and achieved the so-called "imperishable fame."

Against her wishes, Bat Zor found herself beginning to sing. "Your name will surely be forgot / And mine above all glorified / Achieved, have I, what I long sought / The fame which does not ever fade / The glory which shall never die."

As the song echoed through the air, the darkness in the hill became suffocating. Bat Zor felt like a hundred different eyes were glaring at her. She looked to the skies and saw shapes swirling above her, dark bat-like things with wings of the night. Then they vanished in an eye's blink. They had been mere delusions, wild fancies of an injured mind.

As the caravan of food began to arrive and cheers of joy erupted through the camp—as warriors awakened to the glorious flour, fish and meat—Bat Zor shut her eyes and entered a trance.

Searching through the camp, she peered into people's minds, removing their barriers like a lid and examining their contents. Searching for the correct one, she passed by many, then focused on one: a girl from Tharta, correct, but this one was a prostitute. *When will they pay me?* she was thinking. *They said they would pay me.* Bat Zor left the mind of Amarodora and searched on.

She focused on another female, a girl—an Eloesian—who

had married a Fharese man of great import. But no—this Theokrita was married to a satrap. She was asleep, dreaming of the bright blue seas off the coast of Eloesus and her happy island home. This Theokrita must have tired of her husband to dream so fervently and vividly of her childhood.

After scouring more minds, through the surprising variety of Eloesian girls in the Fharese camp, she was ready to give up. *This is the last one,* she thought as she peeled back the mind's defenses and looked within.

This girl—no, a woman of advanced years—was trying to sleep but failing. Guilt and disgust with herself were causing her to toss and turn. She felt ashamed to have lain with her companion—not a husband—a man of immense power in the Fharese world. This woman hailed from Isteros, a place mocked and scorned by true Eloesians. Her accent made her the butt of ridicule wherever she went. She had tried earnestly, for years, to speak in the High Thartan dialect but never mastered it.

Bat Zor read these strands of thought and peeled back deeper, diving further and further into this woman's brain. Sifting through the matter, Bat Zor uncovered the woman's connection to this very hill. She had never been here, but her mind and heart were touched by Kronos. Lord Kronos, she called him. She and other "old believers" in Tharta had gathered in dark places, in city gardens and dim-lit streets, speaking with open scorn at the priests and the temples of the "new gods." This woman had been introduced to her dark faith by a beggar on a street corner. The beggar had been huddled on the twisting streets of Sun God's Wharf, offering knowledge and sacred mysteries.

And this woman, whom Bat Zor was examining, had enlisted the help of her husband King Gygax—for Kronos wanted blood. Assassins had been sent to kill a man named Theron but he had survived them all.

Bat Zor gasped and nearly lost her concentration. This was the woman she had been searching for—Thelema, the disgraced Queen of Tharta.

Without skipping a breath she re-focused and dug deeper, reading the strands of memory, of thought, of opinion, of time. This woman's children were not her husband's, but of a fellow Kronos worshipper. The worshipper had—until recently—been bothering her, telling her of Kronos' need for a blood sacrifice. Now her children were dead.

Deeper and deeper, Bat Zor would have probed, but her mind—in an instant—was swallowed with panic. All rational thought disappeared. She was screaming but no sound emerged from her lips.

The snake had, at long last, gotten to her. A pity Bat Zor could not wring all the secrets from her mind before she had gone.

In the early dawn, Bat Zor made her way to the Royal Tent. A pair of Rephathites, tall and stocky, were guarding the entryway; they let her by without a word.

Inside the tent, many worried faces greeted Bat Zor, many fearful glances, many terrified looks—and the atmosphere of tension was thick. Bat Zor could sense the dread like a cloud, hovering all about—and emanating from the King of Kings' residence.

Bat Zor entered through the tent flap. She fell to her knees. Through the veil, she could sense her husband's boiling rage. This had not been a good idea. She thought of turning to leave—but that would only anger him more. It was not beyond the King of Kings' purview to murder his chief wife; all laws were written by him, and all laws could be broken by him.

"My Mirzanēs," Bat Zor said softly.

"I expect little of a Shakrathite," he said. "In fact, I expect nothing. But I expect much from a wife."

"I am sorry… what do you think I've done—?"

"Silence!" Mirzanēs screamed. "I am not finished, woman! You think I am a fool. You think I do not know your secrets. You are wrong… your powers of sorcery are something I have chosen to overlook. A wiser man would have burned you as a witch, as is deserved. But this—*this*—changes everything."

"What changes everything?"

"Do not think I am a fool!" Mirzanēs shouted. She could sense his anger; it was overwhelming, overpowering—all-consuming. His hands were quaking. His wrath bordered on murderous.

Panicked, Bat Zor thought of running. But her husband the King of Kings had eyes everywhere, all around the world; she would be found out if she fled. Desperately, she summoned all her powers; she reached into his mind, opening it like a clay pot. She tried to soothe it, but the anger and hate had formed an impenetrable barrier. She could not overcome it.

Mirzanēs ripped open the veil. His normally pallid face had turned a bright shade of red. His black eyes were bulging. "Your servant, the serpent—whom you bewitched—has completed its task. It has taken my lover Thelema! It has snuffed out her life! Are you happy?"

Yes, Bat Zor wanted to say. *I am so very happy.* How could he betray her so? How could he forget all these decades they had spent together? How could he spurn her for an Eloesian whore, and a worshipper of demons at that? "I did not send that snake," Bat Zor said. "The gods must have sent it. Bel-Nohai in heaven must have smelled my sacrifices… he must have heard my prayers.

"And yes, I am happy… so happy…"

Like a tiger pouncing on prey, Mirzanēs—sixty-nine years

old—leapt upon her and began savaging her with blows. One fist struck her cheek. She cried out; her cheekbone shuddered but did not break. Another blow broke her nose with a loud crack. She wailed in pain. Now lying on the floor, now bleeding, the blows did not stop, the furious punches did not end. Her old body could not withstand these bruisings; her mind and heart could not bear this hatred.

Soon he began punching her body. Something snapped; she groaned with pain.

And like that, Mirzanēs was sobbing, weeping onto her chest. His tears soaked through her *thawab*, to her undergarments, to her skin. Bat Zor peered into his mind, sensing regret, sensing despair, sensing sorrow. His love coexisted with his anger. There was fury in his mind, but no hate. There was guilt for bedding Thelema; but there was no love for Thelema, only lust. Bat Zor wrapped her arms around him as he sobbed. Her body was bruised and broken. She did not know if she could forgive him.

PORT URSA, JOGHEIRA

The first signs of summer's end had begun. More clouds were seen in the sky, a few wispy white tufts floating across the sea of blue. As Kora stood in Port Ursa, the waves were battering the docks with more strength than before; and a cold wind was steadily gusting from the east. The winds were shifting; the seas would soon become unsafe to sail.

And these southrons were wise sailors. Their dhows and their great warships with a dozen lateen sails had begun to filter in, to cram the too-small harbor of Port Ursa. They knew the seas well; the open waters were their homes.

Worse yet, Kora had observed more and more of them in Port Ursa. Kora and her fellow amazons had, for a long time, believed Eloesians were arrogant. "The people of the mainland," Kora's friends had said, "think so highly of themselves; and they live against the laws of nature."

Yes, the laws of nature were broken by Eloesians; men were leaders and not women. Women stayed at home and not men. Yet these southrons were a cut above in their vast arrogance. They ordered southron women around like chattel. Even amazon women they treated with scorn. Amazon women—who could break their bones and beat them handily in combat—they viewed as subhuman, second to men in all ways.

Kora observed a southron in a turban shouting at a female slave. *At least,* Kora thought, *the Eloesians have a reason for pride.* The Eloesians had defeated the amazons in what they called the Amazon War. The Eloesians had driven the amazons from the mainland, forcing them to take shelter in the islands—Jogheira, Straiteira, Agathë and others.

These southrons, these "Fharese"—had done none of it. Yet the amazons of Port Ursa endured their abuse and wickedness, knowing they could not defeat the Fharese Empire handily. When these southrons cursed the amazons, when their hearts were filled with such dark pride, Kora's people ignored them.

Kora's blood boiled at the thought of it. She had sunfire and a spiked club at her fingertips. Could she not bludgeon that man in the turban, cursing and heckling—against the laws of nature—that woman? Could she not burn him to ash with a splash of sunfire? Did she not have the power of the sun at her fingertips?

Kora had always displayed remarkable self-control; never before had her temper gotten out of hand. But these wicked southrons were pushing her to the breaking point. They were pushing her rage to levels she had never felt before. Perhaps resistance was impossible.

She shut her eyes; she felt the sun's warmth and reveled in its brightness and joy-giving light. She breathed deeply, smelled the warm air scented with rosebushes and sea salt. The sun gave the very earth its light—that is what had been taught at the Solar Temple. In the warmth of the sun, how could she give into anger? How could she be anything but placid?

Slowly, she felt herself calm down. Her heart stopped its quick beating; the boiling of her blood turned to a simmer. In the sun, her anger was quieted. In the sun, giver of life, she could think clearly.

When she opened her eyes, her calm was tested again. A warrior in a white cotton turban was shoving an elderly amazon out of the way. Not only were these southrons rude, they were loud—shouting and cursing at each other and at the strangers hosting them. For days, Port Ursa had stunk of pipes, and a haze of smoke had formed, drifting in from the inns and the homes where the southrons had boarded.

Strong drink was viewed with ill favor—these proud southrons turned up their noses at firewater—but the stench of pipes, the hacking and coughing, the pungent odor, all that was acceptable.

At the thought of firewater—a thick and powerful burst of flavor—Kora's mouth watered. She could drink her sisters under the table. A gulp of that and the anger—already returning—would dissipate.

She could not bear to stand in Port Ursa a moment longer. She had a boat and a host of handmaids ready to paddle oars. She could escape this isle, just yet—perhaps find an isle of her own. She would leave Jogheira and all the disappointments behind.

~

The Triton's Spear was a bireme, equipped with two rows of oars and two square sails. Kora, as one of the most senior Solarine, and a wealthy landowner at that, could afford her. A ship as fine as the *Triton*, with a staff to row it, was out of reach of all but the most wealthy. Kora counted it as a blessing of the gods that she owned such a treasure as well as enough handmaids to set sail.

One by one, her handmaids filtered below-decks. When they finally shoved off the pier and entered the bright blue waters of the sea, Kora took her place at the bow. She exhaled and breathed a soft sigh of relief as the ship carried her away from Jogheira, away from Amazonia, away from the troubles that plagued the world. War and bloodshed was the order of the day; but here on the open seas, no one could touch Kora. The waves might claim her—but the Fharese couldn't.

That thought vanished at the sight of a Fharese armada—a dozen dhows of varying size, from small crafts to towering warships, heading south-by-southeast into the mainland.

As *The Triton's Spear* gained speed, slicing through the waves, the familiar small islands around Jogheira beckoned to Kora.

These tiny islands had no place on a map; no one lived on them. They were free from Amazonian politics. They were free from the southrons.

Off the coast of one island, a siren was sunning on a rock. Her webbed hands were outstretched and her fin was splashing in the water. She was singing, as all sirens did; but her song was soft and faint. A siren—if she wanted—could sing so loudly and beautifully that sailors could hear her for a mile around. She would draw them in, even invite one onto her rock—then grab him and drag him down into the depths.

Such lessons, a sailor learned from his earliest days, when he was plying his trade. *Do not listen to the siren's call.* It was as fundamental as never taking shelter in an isle you do not recognize. A sailor on a strange island was liable to become a cyclops' dinner. How many sailors had been devoured by the hulking one-eyed giants—the cyclops, the sons of chaos? Yet Kora had no fear. How could a stupid, inbred giant be any worse than a southron?

Yes, hatred had consumed her. Was death not better than humiliation?

Three dhows were sailing by in the distance. The setting sun was glaring red on their lateen sails.

And then it struck her.

Queen Daphnë had disappointed Kora utterly. Daphnë had betrayed her calling, her one duty to protect the amazon people. Yet her hand could be forced.

If Daphnë would not declare war on these woman-hating southrons, Kora would force her to. *Yes, yes.* She would lose the *Triton* in the process. But that was a small price to pay. "Turn around!" Kora shouted. "Turn around! Back to Tigris!"

~

The moon and stars were out when they finally docked. Kora ordered her handmaids to return home.

Fharese dhows—hundreds of them—were crammed in every conceivable spot in Tigris' harbor. She left the safety of the *Triton*, never questioning what she was about to do. An act such as this—for any woman less than Kora's standing—would warrant death. Even for a woman of Kora's standing, her plans could end in execution. But Kora could not bear to see her people humiliated. She would force a war, with or without Daphnë's help.

Out of the shadows emerged Ahmett. The so-called "emir of Bajir" had the familiar smirk on his face. "Kora," he scoffed. "I recognize those eyes."

A retinue of warriors with sabers stood behind him.

"Do you know that I have forbidden all ships to leave, save our dhows?" Ahmett said. "You have broken the law."

Kora felt her fists clenching of her own accord. The sun's warmth and brightness could not calm her now. Anger was growing; pressure was building in her veins.

"I know this pitiful kingdom has little to offer," Ahmett said. "Believe me; I have seen the bazaars of Bezakirah and the Grand Fire Temple of Taifun. In comparison, the north is a desolate place. Your heart yearns to leave; but it is against the law."

From her side, Kora drew her spiked club—a bulky work of wrought-iron which every full Solarine carried.

"Ha! She intends to threaten me," said Ahmett, "but she cannot. Her old heart is full of hate; but she knows the Fharese Empire is too great for her."

I can still back down, thought Kora. *I can still change course, and perhaps preserve my life.* "Once, the amazons were a great power," Kora said. "Unrivaled, in fact. We have grown weak and accustomed to defeat. But I cannot bear your insults anymore. I will force a war... even if my people will perish in the attempt, at least we will perish with our pride."

In an eye's blink, Kora vaulted herself forward, bringing her spiked club to bear on Ahmett's turbaned head. His skull split open with a loud crack, sending bits of bone, flesh and brain in the air. The warriors piled on after her with shouts of rage. They slashed with their sabers but Kora, kicking and swinging, killed three in as many blows. The ten fought on bravely; but after she sent another to the ground with a skull-crushing blow, they turned and ran, screaming into the night.

Kora wiped some of the blood and flesh from her mouth. She had broken out with a cold sweat. Her old bones were not accustomed to such exertion. In her youth, during the conflict with the Agathë Islanders, she had killed a hundred-and-thirteen enemy warriors—even one of their chieftains, by the name of Black Phoebë. But this old body of hers had not seen combat since then. How quickly the rhythm of battle returned, how quickly the hard-won wisdom.

Then again, she was battling *men*—not much of a challenge.

The next part of her plan would ensure a war. There was no going back now. A war had already started, for better or worse: Ahmett, the emir of Bazijirah or whatever flea-ridden outpost he came from, had been slain by one of the queen's chief women.

As she walked down the dock, she began her work. Calling up her powers of magic, she drew the power of the sun—available to her even in the moonlight—and tossed a splash of bright fire onto the deck of a mighty dhow.

Instantly the dhow caught fire, becoming—within seconds—a blazing inferno so hot it immediately spread to the docks. Kora did not run; instead, she quickened her pace slightly. She walked by another dhow and drew up the sun's power again, tossing more sunfire onto its vulnerable wood. Again, flame consumed it, devouring the wood as only sunfire could.

More dhows soon caught fire as the blaze spread. *The Triton's Spear* would surely not escape the inferno; but what were all those thousands of gold pieces she had spent worth, compared to the pride of the amazon nation?

By the time she reached the harbor, day had replaced night; the darkness was dispelled in the red light of the raging flame. There were screams coming from Port Ursa. Surprise and panic was overtaking everyone, amazon and southron. For now, no one realized what the fire meant; the southrons' king would not forgive.

War would follow, great and terrible. Wars upon wars, until the end.

KORTHICA-THARTICA BORDER

When the battle lines of the Fharese appeared, a shiver passed through Ardyo that he couldn't shake. He had led these sixty-six thousand free men to their deaths. They had chosen this bitter cup of their own accord, but had Ardyo done everything he could to convince them otherwise. Perhaps he could have explained it in a different way, in a more persuasive way, to change their minds.

Yet they had refused him. "No," one "hoplite" had said—a man from Thénai—a sandalmaker who now served as the supposed commander of his battalion. "I would rather die than become some magi's slave."

The common people of Eloesus did not know much about Fharas, or anything at all. They did not know that, if they surrendered, they in all likelihood would be allowed to continue their lives. No one would become a magus's slave. But now that they had resisted, neither Korthos or Tharta would be shown mercy. Now, because they had dared resist the King of Kings, the cities would be razed to their foundations; the men beheaded with Fharese sabers; the women and children, sold into bondage.

Some women—the young and the beautiful—would become concubines in the King of Kings' harem. Most would become the slaves of rich Fharese women. And yet the women of Korthos and Thénai—as Ardyo had seen—were equally defiant as the men. Law forbade women to take up arms and serve as hoplites; but if such restrictions were lifted, surely they would be here too—marching with their husbands, brothers and fathers.

Behind the countless Fharese warriors with their sabers and wicker shields, the giant forms of elephants appeared, trunks painted some shade of crimson. Row after row of chariots rattled behind the Fharese warriors.

Eventually they stopped, when they were close enough to see the whites of their eyes.

Ardyo recalled the moment just days ago when the Arkadian had brought him gifts. He still had the hyacinth, dead and wilted, in his pocket. He would keep it close to him until the end—until a Fharese saber struck him down and he joined his wife Mykalë beneath the earth, in the Fields of Paradise. Surely that is where she resided now, beside her equals Phillipidēs and Helēmon. There, in those happy fields, the grief that had characterized her life would be gone and banished. "Someday," Ardyo whispered to the grass, which had its roots in the underworld. "Someday soon I will join you, sweet Mykalë."

He could not forget her, not as long as he lived. Here, in the camp, hoplites had to subsist on stewed beans and other meager fare. Even the beans reminded him of sweet Mykalë.

Months after her death, a mad philosopher had wandered the streets of Korthos, threatening to kill anyone who sold beans. "Beans are the souls of the dead!" he had screamed to anyone who would listen. "The souls sprout up from the underworld—they are contained in this thing you eat! Do not destroy these souls, you barbarians!" This mad philosopher Galeios had gained his fair share of disciples—but within weeks, he had been murdered by one of them.

"Be with me, sweet Mykalë," he whispered to the grass. "I will join you soon." Whether in the Fields of Paradise or the pale fires of hell, he would see her soon.

A MILE FROM KORTHOS

The road from Kersepoli to Korthos was long, two-hundred miles from one end to the other. The Sun King's Road, it was called, though Pherion did not know why.

The Kersepolan portion, covering about half, was bare dirt—but Korthos, ever wealthy and wise, had paved their portion with gleaming white stone. Yet as Kersepoli's territory expanded ever further and further, more and more of that gleaming white road was under their control.

In his pack he had stuffed the lightning orb, which in ancient days—he learned—had been called the Cnidos Mechanism after the island where it was found. The book he had pocketed on the way out had explained as much: the Cnidos Mechanism had been discovered by a group of Thenoan sailors. Thinking it useless, they sold it for scrap metal at the price of ten silver *doukon* to a Korthian inventor. Like all things Korthian, the city of Kersepoli had stolen it from him.

Five days into the journey, as Pherion rode along at his breakneck pace, funerary monuments began to appear along the road. Rich Korthians—guildmasters, priests, merchants and landowners—had erected grand tombs. Once, he had asked King Kyrion why knowing they'd be dead and rotting, people built grand pyramids and mausoleums for themselves.

"Because," Kyrion had told him, "there is only one true way to eternal life—and that is to be remembered forever."

The tales of the underworld—the Fields of Paradise where Phillipidēs and Helēmon lived in bliss; the River of Souls; and the Lake of Fire—did strike Pherion as unbelievable. But he still believed in the gods—in Tyros, in Alabastros, and especially Amara the Mother. Perhaps it was folly, but how could something come from nothing, except by the gods' help?

Perhaps it was not up to him to decide.

~

The gate of Korthos was shut. Archers were posted above the towering walls, wearing green capes over their backs and green horsehair crests on their helmets.

These walls were even taller than Kersepoli's, and made of finer, more perfectly-fitted stone. Not only was height considered in the walls' making, but also beauty.

"I come from Kersepoli!" Pherion shouted as loud as he could. The chief archer was glaring at him. "I come bearing a great gift… something that could help in the war effort!"

The chief archer barked some order. Within minutes, the gears and wheels behind the gate were twisting, and opened the massive doorway just enough to let Pherion inside.

~

Korthos was as Pherion had seen in his youth. The white-paved streets were lined with limestone temples, pillared mansions and quiet gardens. The riches from a hundred colonies across the Middle Sea had poured into the mother city, allowing for the construction of grand monuments and great works of stone. Above the streets, on the towering High City, the temple to Arephon lord of thunder and lightning reminded all citizens of their patron god. Yet other gods were worshipped here.

The main street opened up into the so-called Heaven's Square with its myriad temples. In one corner was the temple to "Alabastros the King." In another was a temple to "Victorious Tyros." Another temple towered above the others with three stories—the temple of "All the Gods." Each story of this temple had different columns: at the bottom Thenoan columns, simple and bulky; in the middle Korthian with their ornate fluting and curled scroll-like capitals; at the top Megarine, with thin bodies and capitals decorated in leaves and flowers.

Yet Heaven's Square was almost empty now. Some women were buying and selling, and some old men—whoever could not fight in the war effort—but the vivacity and liveliness of Heaven's Square was gone. Beyond the Temple of Nix and the Temple of Alabastros the King, beyond the woman selling wine bottles and the woman selling purple cloth, there was the House of Assembly. A hoplite battalion was posted outside. In a happier time, such a show of force would be unnecessary.

A statue lurked outside the House of Assembly. Built of mixed bronze and iron in the form of a hoplite, its head stretched to the height of the House of Assembly's roof. Pherion stopped and stared. The statue's eyes were made of some crystalline substance. A wire stretched from the tip of its bronze helm. And in some places—where the plates of bronze did not cover—there were gears and wheels. This was not a statue, but a war machine.

Pherion could not believe it. Were the Korthians truly this ingenious?

After explaining his purpose, the hoplites at the door let him inside.

~

The seats in the House of Assembly—stone rows in a horseshoe-like shape surrounding a speaking floor—were mostly empty. A few old men in chitons sat down, speaking amongst themselves. On the speaking floor, a white-haired demiarch was chatting with a man in a turban and a long white robe. What was a southron doing in the Korthian House of Assembly?

Pherion approached them forcefully, without any cares about protocol. "Where is your archon?" he snapped, overwhelmed at the situation, unsure of what to make of it.

The southron turned his yellowed eyes to Pherion. His gaze dripped with arrogance and derision. The demiarch turned to Pherion as well. "Who are you?" he snapped.

"I come from—" Pherion stopped himself. This situation had become unpredictable and he wasn't sure what all to make of it. It seemed to him the darkest possibility of all—that the Korthians were surrendering to the southrons—seemed likely. "I must speak to him. I have a gift worth many thousands of gold pieces. It belongs to him—I must return it."

The demiarch pursed his lips. "Hector is in the temple of Isdar with his Fharese counterpart."

So it is true.

"Near Heaven's Square, on Laurel Street, behind the Temple of All Gods."

Pherion looked into the southron's jaundiced eyes. Surely there was some innocent explanation. Surely these southrons had defected from their brethren. Surely the Korthians had not surrendered—and all hope was not lost.

Unsure, he returned to the stables where he had kept his horse. He removed the Cnidos Mechanism from his pack and laid it quietly into the horse's saddlebags. He could not chance anything. He could not afford to make a mistake and plunge Eloesus into disaster. He still did not understand what use the lightning orb had; but could he risk letting it fall into the hands of the southrons?

Returning to Heaven's Square and the three-tiered Temple

of All Gods—together with its Korthian, Thenoan and Megarine columns—he walked on ahead, down the white-paved but mostly empty streets. As he walked on in the shadow of the titanic building, the sound of music appeared—plucking lyres and cascading harps, together with singing and loud laughter. The temple of Isdar lay just behind.

The marble building was built according to all the customs of the Megarine order. Its triangular pediment roof was flanked on all sides by tall Megarine columns—slender, white, exotic, decorated at their capitals with leaves and flowers. Below the triangular pediment roof—itself ornamented with bright red shingles—was a frieze, set against a blue background, depicting naked dancers and white tigers. From its open double doors, it was clear the music and laughter radiated from within.

Isdar—goddess of passion, eroticism and lust—was considered a southron import. Priests of other gods looked down on her, even went as far as to call her evil. Pherion had never been to one of her temples before, nor did he ever have the desire. There was enough lust in this world—enough ladies of the evening, prowling the streets; enough courtesans in scarlet gowns and gold hairpieces. Why did there need to be a goddess of passion in addition to all that?

He passed through the doors and was greeted by a pair of tiger statues, painted white with black stripes and yellow eyes so ornate, Pherion feared they would come alive to devour him.

Past another set of double doors, also open, and he entered a vast room.

The music, so loud it strained his ears, was played by the deft hands of courtesans. Holding scarlet cloths that covered only a portion of their bodies, they managed to play their instruments despite the attentions of the patrons—two strumming giant harps; another curled on the couch with a nude southron as she plucked away at a lyre, giggling.

Two other courtesans were dancing nude on a stage, twisting and heaving around a pair of white Megarine columns. Pherion could not help but feel his body respond; against his best wishes these beautiful women, scarcely clothed, were awakening lust in him. Their shapely bodies, their bare wastes, their uncovered bosoms, were filling him with desire.

A hand poked him. Pherion gasped and blushed with embarrassment. A courtesan stood there, holding an ivory bowl. "My good man… a donation of five *doukon* to the goddess and you may have me, all day and all night."

Pherion blushed even further. He would not dignify her words with a response. Instead he turned and scanned the room, searching for the archon Hector and his southron companion.

A nude woman sat on a swing which swayed from one end of the room to the other. She was singing:

> *The queen of love does greet you…*
> *The queen of love does wrap you*
> *In her warm and soft embrace…*

But this was not love, it was basest passion.

At last, in a lonely corner, covered in the shadows of the room, he spied gray-haired Hector and a southron. Neither Hector nor the southron had glasses of wine—a key feature of any lust-filled visit to Isdar's temple. Instead, they were picking pine-nuts from a bowl and popping them into their mouths at random intervals.

The little doubt Pherion had was melting away. Somehow, these Korthians had backed away on their promises. Bit by bit their resolve was crumbling. They would be slaves to the Fharese at the end of it; of that, Pherion was sure.

Still he approached, holding out hope. Hector turned to look at him; the southron followed, revealing a face of dusky complexion with harsh-angled features and a thin black beard. He wore a cotton headwrap that bore the dirt and wear of many desert travails. A saber was strapped to his side, curved in southron fashion.

"Hector," Pherion said. He would not bother with any formality or reverence that he himself did not feel. "I come from Kersepoli."

"That I can see," Hector answered, "from your long and womanly hair."

Pherion bit back an insult. The southron laughed. At least the Kersepolans did not flinch from battle—King Kyrion's Kersepolans, at least. "I came bearing a gift," said Pherion, "which would help in the war effort."

Hector's mocking smile faded.

"I can see, however, that there is no need of it. You have already surrendered."

The archon glared. "Surrendered? No such thing. What have you brought us—"

"Pherion," he said. He, like other Kersepolans, did not value deceit. Lying was not a skill that was taught—not even to Kersepolan politicians, not even to Kersepolan kings.

"Well?" said the archon. "Go on. Saana is a defector from the Fharese army. Do you truly think I would send the Free and Democratic Army of Korthos to fight a war and then abandon them?"

He had a point. And though Pherion did not trust this Saana at all, it was perfectly plausible. Perhaps the Fharese army had proven weak; after all, the five-hundred Chosen had slain countless thousands. "The Cnidos Mechanism."

Something about the archon's stunned surprise, something about the subtle twist of his smile—made Pherion think that, perhaps, he had made a grave mistake. This Hector was collaborating somehow, with this Saana. Saana had promised to leave the archon in power. He had promised him something. *No, I am overthinking. Not every smirk and smile has a meaning.*

"Ah, this will help greatly in our war effort." The archon's eyes met the southron's gaze in a way Pherion did not like. "The colossus has been near-useless… but now… now…"

At the word "colossus" Pherion knew instantly what he meant—the titanic bronze statue sitting idle in the Korthian square.

"You must show me," said the archon. "You must show me at once!"

The command erased all doubt from Pherion's mind that this archon—this Hector—was a schemer to the core, and meant nothing of what he said. He was in full collaboration with the Fharese.

Pherion ducked away and bolted out of the temple as fast as he could.

"Arrest him!" Hector called after him. "Arrest that man!"

The number of southrons in the city became evident as Pherion ran down the way. The crowd of warriors—some in turbans and some in cotton headwraps—grew as he turned down every street. They could not catch him; Pherion had been the fastest runner in his battalion and one of the fastest of the five-hundred Chosen. Three times he had won the laurel wreath in the sprint during the Games.

He reached the stable quicker than he expected. He was panting and dripping in sweat as he drove away the stable boys and sent them running. He yanked open the stable door, reached into the saddlebag, felt the cold brass of the Cnidos Mechanism—and then saw southrons pouring into the stables, sabers drawn.

Without another thought, Pherion leapt up on the unsaddled horse and urged it on unsteadily. It took off at a gallop, driving through the ranks of the southrons, crushing their chests with its hooves.

On he ran, and the southrons did not have time to react as the horse bull-rushed through them, trampling underfoot. As Pherion galloped forward, he grabbed the cold metal of the Cnidos Mechanism and hoisted it in the crook of his arm.

Soon he reached Heaven's Square, and an army of southrons had followed him. In the far corner of the square, the archon Hector was pointing to him and screaming: "There is the man! There is the man!"

Pherion galloped ahead until he was in the colossus' shadow. He spied a ladder going up into the body of the statue, just out of his reach.

He leapt up off the horse and just managed to catch a rung. He pulled himself up the ladder just as the southron warriors arrived—thousands and thousands of them, crowding Heaven's Square. Arrows began to fly as Pherion heaved himself to safety within the well-armored body of the mighty colossus.

When he reached the end of the surprisingly-exhausting climb, it became evident he had reached the head of the statue. Through a narrow visor he could see the southrons swarming the square. Arrows were loosed but they bounced off uselessly against the colossus' bronze skin.

On a metal panel, there were controls—a leather-bound stick and several buttons. Pherion puzzled for a while, wondering how on earth this Cnidos Mechanism was supposed to help. He guessed there was some socket or hollow hole where it was meant to go—but he could not see any.

Southron warriors were beating the colossus with clubs. Though having no success, surely—with enough pressure and vicious blows—they could bring the machine down. He scanned the tiny room, seeing an iron rod which shot up through the colossus's head and presumably, outside. There was a bare stool parked in front of the panel.

The clanking sound of southrons climbing the ladder sent Pherion into a panic. He slammed the trapdoor shut and locked it; the Cnidos Mechanism went flying and hit the floor, compressing the button and calling up its powers—the metal skin folded away, and a blazing bolt of lightning appeared; the beam caught on to the iron rod and the very colossus itself seemed to blaze with energy.

A cosmic shout emerged from the colossus: a loud chorus of a cry like the voice of a god. The colossus lurched forward as it took its first step; Pherion fell down and skidded across the floor as its head moved with it. Giddy, he took his seat on the stool—fused to the floor of the cockpit. He grasped the lever and pushed it forward; the colossus lurched forward in the direction he pushed. He hit a button and a blast of searing fire issued from the colossus's eyes—a fire that broke up the stone of Heaven's Square and caused the very stone itself to burn. The southrons were screaming now; many had been charred to ash by this "death ray."

He pressed the button again, and another chunk of Heaven's Square exploded in a white burst of light. A chunk of the once-ornate stonework hit the colossus head on, but the colossus did not so much as buckle. Many southrons were burnt to dust; others, having caught fire, screamed and ran wild.

Slowly but surely the immense colossus, the titanic masterwork of Eloesian ingenuity, marched on—crushing the bones of southrons as it walked, breaking up the elaborate stone of Heaven's Square.

Pherion zapped the death ray freely, driving southrons away, but common Korthian citizens—among them many women—had taken up arms and were cutting down the cowards as they ran.

Pherion yanked the control-lever and turned the colossus completely around. He blasted the death ray, shattering stone and catching southron warriors on fire. Again and again he blasted the ray, slaying hundreds of southrons with each blinding burst. Buildings had begun to burn; smoke was rising like out of hell's abyss. But Pherion no longer thought of Korthos; he was directing the colossus out of the gates, which it would surely shatter. He would take the colossus where it was most useful, and needed: to the most important battle of his time, to the place that would decide the fate of centuries. To the battlefields of Fharas and Eloesus he would take it—and if death met him there, he would greet her bravely.

THE WHITE TIGER THRONE, TIGRIS

A length of cloth had been undignifiedly tied around Kora's mouth. Her old hands had been cinched in coarse rope behind her back. She had been displayed like a war captive before Queen Daphnë's throne. Such a treatment would mean death; it showed both Kora's vulnerability and the hatred fixed upon her. But Kora knew better. Daphnë would not have Kora slain. Their friendship was deeper than the total calamity Kora had brought upon the amazon nation. Their bond could not be broken—not even by the disaster looming just ahead.

Daphnë had left her gold scepter behind, and instead had a glaive and a pair of chakrams. With anyone besides Kora, it would suggest imminent execution—as did the fury in Daphnë's eyes. "I cannot believe I ever called you friend," she said.

How luminous did her feathered headdress appear in the torchlight. How many parrots and egrets and cranes had been plucked of their feather for its making?

"You are not worried," Daphnë said. "You think you will get special treatment because you were my friend… because, until today, I had love for you. But those days are gone… gone with those burning ships, those murdered southrons."

Port Ursa had become the scene of a great massacre; blood stained those streets, where thousands of southrons had been slain. Kora had not seen such gore since her youth, when the amazons of Agathë tried to break free from the queen and war had consumed them all. It was a precursor of what was to come—whether Daphnë wanted it or not.

"Do you understand the danger you have put us in?" Daphnë asked. "The southrons' king has declared the war 'will not be over until every last amazon is slain.' Now war is unavoidable. And we will lose."

"War is unavoidable," said Kora. "But whether we lose is up to you."

Daphnë kicked her in the face. "Do not think I will have mercy on you, traitor."

Kora, bristling from the hard leather boot, blinked away her tears of pain. Daphnë would not slay her; she would not lay a hand on her head. "It is our last chance," Kora said. "Our last task for this world. We amazons must rise to the challenge of our day."

Daphnë spat in Kora's face. "The golden age has passed, Kora. My task as queen is to manage our decline… to ensure our mere survival. You have threatened this task, Kora. You have threatened everything. With your pride and hubris, you have ensured our total destruction."

"Unless we join with the mainlanders and defeat these southrons," Kora answered. "Unless we learn to fight again… and believe that, for the amazon people, there are better days ahead— that we still have a place in *this* world and not just the last."

The fury in Daphnë's eyes vanished, replaced with tears. "If only I had your hope. Your foolish hope. You must die, Kora… for this, you must die…"

"You may kill me," said Kora, "but the war has already begun. You may fight it with me or without me…"

Tears soon flowed down Daphnë's dark cheeks. "There is no future for our people, Kora…"

"That is what you say," Kora answered.

"The seas are full of enemy warships…"

"But we have the gold arks… and the Juggernaut." Kora observed Daphnë's surprise. As queen, she knew of the gold arks— the mighty warships of the amazon fleet—and of the Juggernaut, the largest and mightiest ship the world had yet seen. Yet these words had obviously not been spoken to her throughout all her young life; the invulnerability of the amazon fleet was a fact, but an ignored one. The thought of amazons starting a war—a people in decline whose best days were long past—was unthinkable. The power of the amazon navy had thus become irrelevant.

"Oh, Kora…" Daphnë answered.

"There are twenty thousand braves on Jogheira… and summoning them will be easy. The beacon fires will draw them to Tigris…"

"The beacon fires have not been lit in three hundred years."

"But they can be lit now," said Kora.

Daphnë answered Kora's bold words with silence. *She is mad*, she was surely thinking. *This old hag has lost her mind.* But Kora had not lost her mind. All this she had orchestrated with careful planning… all this, to force Daphnë to do the right thing.

"Then we will march," Daphnë said. "It may well be the end. But one last war will be fought… one last battle, one last stand. The amazons will have one final day of glory before they fade away…"

The bunched twigs and logs at the top of Magdala's Tower had been replaced out of custom; and many so-called fire tenders had viewed their duty as a religious one. But that afternoon, the word was given—and the fire tender tossed a burning torch onto the oil-soaked wood. Its blaze was sudden and brilliant, so searing hot that the fire tender fell away carelessly and almost dropped to his death.

Within minutes, the fires blazed on the outlying towers miles away—forming brilliant beacons on the horizon.

From those towers, other beacons were lit—the amazons of Wolf's Creek and Lizard's Thicket took up their glaives. The shepherdesses of Outer Tigria made arrangements for hired hands, then grabbed their glaives and helms.

Beacons blazed on from there, spreading from Tigria to outlying villages and cities, and to barren wilds where hardly an amazon lived. Within an hour, the beacons had reached the tower at Ipsos on Jogheira's far western end, one hundred miles away; and the amazons of that ancient city raised their glaives and cheered. There, in Ipsos, the Solarine of the Grand Sun Temple lit braziers in the Sun's Circle and raised their spiked clubs in celebration. By nightfall, amazon warriors dressed for battle were pouring out of city gates from Ipsos to Tigris, from Kleomenë to Kolkis. Gold arks were sent across the sea to light beacon fires on the isles of Straiteira and Agathë; and more arks were sent on the long journey to Kalormenë and the isles surrounding Delphidia.

Soon twenty thousand warriors from Jogheira would meet in the royal city of Tigris; together with thirty-thousand from Straiteira and as many as ten thousand from Agathë and Kalormenë.

The armies of the amazons would gather for one last stand, for the sake of Amara the Battle Maiden, for Mira the Illumined One, and for the sun herself.

FRONT LINES, KORTHICA-THARTA BORDER

The phalanx was a funny thing.

The Free and Democratic Armies of Korthos and Thénai were outnumbered at an outrageous scale. Yet Ardyo's hoplites, having locked together their shields, standing in rows eight men deep, had managed to repel the attacks.

Morale hung by a tenuous thread. If one hoplite failed to hold the line, the phalanx would collapse, and these sixty-five thousand young men would lose their lives in a massive slaughter.

The Fharese warriors had broken upon the hoplites like a wave crashing on ocean rocks; like rocks they had stood firm and failed to move. But the sun was beating down on them, and as humans they had limits. Their energy was being sapped away under the weight of the iron helmets and the uncomfortable burden of the bronze breastplates.

As Stratego, Ardyo's helmet was larger, and his horsehair crest was much higher on his head. This had made him the target of many assaults, but blending in with his own army was considered cowardly—unfitting for a Stratego.

The Fharese charged them—a group of a hundred, riding on giant horse. A dozen of them hurled javelins, which shattered upon the hoplites' shields. Spears shot out from the back ranks of Eloesians and impaled the horses before the Fharese could make their attacks.

The air smelled thickly of death and rotting corpses. The noise was causing Ardyo's mind to swim. Vultures circled overhead; they knew a feast was coming. By the end of this battle, those birds would be feasting on Eloesian flesh far more than Fharese. How many Fharese had been slain? Ardyo did not know; whenever the

Fharese suffered a massacre they were replaced with fresh and energetic warriors.

Late in the day, when the sun was low in the sky and the heat had begun to wane, the Fharese drew back. The stinking bodies of their brothers lay there; countless Fharese had been slain but the Eloesian phalanx had not bucked or broken. Out of the army, there was a rustling—then the loud grinding and heavy grating of wheels, chewing up weeds and bushes underfoot.

A great platform was rolling in, drawn by teams of slaves. At the top of the pyramidal stone machine was a man, no shorter than seven feet tall. His body appeared to be of gold, and his eyes were sapphires which glowed in the sunset light. Gold chains drooped from his arms and the sun reflected off his silver boots. He appeared to be a metallic man, though it was surely just a suit— worth the cost of many kingdoms. Motionless he stood as the slaves—naked save for their harnesses—pulled the platform of many tons up to within feet of Ardyo.

At last they relinquished their work and the platform shuddered as it fell still upon the grass.

"Who are you?" Ardyo snapped.

"I am the Voice of the King of Kings; his Voice and his vicar on earth," answered the metallic man. "I am the Voice of a god and the vicar of a god. Fall to your face and worship me."

"The Korthians and the Thenoans will not submit," said Ardyo, "nor will we worship a mere man."

"And yet," said this so-called Voice, "your 'archon' has already submitted to me. Hector has brought out a lamb and sacrificed it to me... to his new god. Korthos has joined my empire."

The way he spoke, the specificity of his words, and Ardyo's knowledge about Hector's character—it all made him certain this Voice spoke the truth. Yet Ardyo had to think about his men. He had to think about how such devastating news would affect them. "You lie!" Ardyo shouted. He signaled, quietly, with his hands, for a javelin.

"Submit to me," said this Voice. "Bring me an offering… of gold, silver, aloes and myrrh. Then take a ewe lamb and sacrifice it before my altar."

Only then did Ardyo notice an altar, fashioned of stone, on the platform where the steps began.

"Join me," the Voice continued, "and I will forgive the deaths you have caused. Surrender your arms and you may work as hired hands to plow my fields… to feed my cities and my armies… to expand my kingdom. Your leader Hector has already seen the light of reason."

"You lie!" Ardyo shouted again. He felt the hard wood of a javelin, pushed into his hand. He had only one chance.

From the folds of his metallic suit, the Voice produced a scroll of lambskin. "I thought you might disbelieve. But here it is, written and sealed." With his finger the Voice broke the wax seal and let it unravel. A document had been signed by two-hundred hands—as many demiarchs served in the House of Assembly. "Korthians!" shouted Ardyo. "Do you accept what our government has done to us?"

"No!" came back the shouts of countless thousands.

Perhaps Ardyo should have been surprised that Hector— after sending the Free and Democratic Army to fight the Fharese— had quickly buckled under the pressure. But it did not surprise him at all. If Korthos was burned and its people were taken slave, how could Hector maintain his status? How could the Politarch of Grain and Wine, or the Politarch of Water and Sanitation hold on to their lucrative positions?

"The matter is finished," shouted the Voice. His metal body gleamed in the sun. "Here is your last chance… to join the empire willingly… to—"

Ardyo, having taken three charging steps forward, hurled the javelin.

It hit home, perfectly striking the Voice's heart—but shattered and broke. The gold had fallen away, laying bare the iron breastplate beneath it.

"So you have chosen the path of death," said the Voice. His calm and rational tone was fraying at the seams. Poisonous anger was seeping through. *How dare these heathens resist the King of Kings,* he was surely thinking. *These pederasts and wastrels, these drunkards and philosophers.* "The path of death!" the Voice continued at a shout. "The path that leads you to your graves… and then perdition. If you will not fall before the King of Kings willingly, we will make you. I shall enjoy watching you die, *adwanīm.*"

The platform began rolling backward. Soon it had disappeared behind the countless ranks of Fharese.

Yes, Ardyo thought. *We have chosen our path.* And it surely led to death. But Ardyo and his men would not suffer on as slaves to the Fharese. Their lives, having been happy and free, would end suddenly. The lives of Hector and those who followed him would continue—gloomy and despairing, floating on like shades in the River of Souls.

Ardyo laid his spear to rest. He fingered the dried-up hyacinth in his pocket. Quietly, to the earth, he whispered to his wife—now gone on to the underworld. *I will join you soon.* Whether in the gloomy river beneath the earth or in the happy fields, he would see sweet Mykalë, his love.

FHARESE CAMP, KORTHICA-THARTICA BORDER

Bat Zor had heard the angry ravings of the emirs and princes. Though none doubted their eventual victory, they were furious that they had to expend such great resources to defeat these Eloesians. The humiliation at Sage Valley, where the five-hundred "Chosen" warriors had slain ten-thousand Fharese, could not be forgotten. Now, as they slowly worked to grind down these so-called "Free and Democratic Armies," furious shouts and angry curses were the order of the day.

A haunting memory was lurking in the back of Bat Zor's mind.

Days ago—or was it weeks?—a young Eloesian man had come to her and offered her a basket. From that basket, a snake had emerged, a snake which had strangled to death her rival. Yet he had also offered her a small bit of wisdom: "Beware your ships; do not take shelter."

She had not spoken of it to anyone. She had spent all her time and energy recovering from her bruised body and heart. It was not easy, in the camp, far from the easy comforts in the palace.

Besides, she had doubted the words. The "Sacred Io," whom the Eloesian had spoken of, was widely considered a madwoman even by her people.

But then a messenger had come in, riding into camp. Bat Zor had been away from her husband's presence for days by then— but news had filtered out. Ships, burning, after having taken shelter in amazon country. *Beware your ships… do not take shelter.*

She knew where this Io lived—on a mountain with a bent

and jagged peak, in view of the town of Arkadion. What other pearls of wisdom did this Io possess—about the war, and about Bat Zor herself? In the darkest moments, when the thought of her broken relationship with Mirzanēs shook her to her core—she thought of donning her riding gear, leaving her black *thawab* behind, and riding away to seek Io's wisdom.

A horn blew. In the distance, where the armies were fighting, the ranks had begun to shift. The enraged emirs and princes had decided on drastic action. But what?

FRONT LINES, KORTHICA-THARTICA BORDER

Ardyo, locked shoulder-to-shoulder with his brothers in arms, watched as a dark shape emerged on the horizon. In size it was taller than the elephants: a tower of wood, set on wheels.

The Fharese warriors began shouting. "The City Crusher!" one shouted.

Moving slower than a human's walk, it ground ahead; as the Fharese lines peeled back Ardyo got a clear view. Each story of the clumsy hundred-foot-tall monstrosity was equipped with a battering ram. A catapult was fixed to its roof. At the bottom, an iron, spiked roller ground its way across the earth and stone.

Pushing this behemoth were two giants—pasty-white, misshapen ogres of men. Immediately Ardyo signaled for javelins. Two-dozen went flying—five hit home, three in one and two in the other. But the giants continued their toil, pushing the City Crusher ahead. The giants did not bleed, only sweated as they drove the machine forward. Javelins were sticking from their arms and chests but they did not care.

The City Crusher was growing closer. Ardyo called for more javelins; they had nearly run out. Again a volley was thrown; even more javelins struck the giants, sticking into them like pincushions, but they only cried out and drove ahead, shouldering this massive burden as if it was their only task in life.

What hellish jungle, what wretched swamp, had these creatures emerged from? What caused these giants to serve the King of Kings?

The last of the javelins were thrown; one struck the City Crusher itself, breaking loose a board and revealing the crowd of warriors inside. The others struck the giants; at last they began to bleed—with black blood—but on and on they went, pushing the siege engine as it ground everything before it underfoot.

Ardyo asked the goddess Amara to strike it down. *Do you care at all for the people who have revered you so?* How many lambs had been offered in her name? How many bulls and heifers? Was the blood insufficient. Ardyo cried out for Amara as the City Crusher blotted out the sun. It was not a hundred feet tall, but two hundred—perhaps a thousand. It put to shame all mountains, even the Mount of Prophecy—and no stone could withstand its spiked roller, devouring and flattening everything underfoot.

The air grew cold; there were loud ecstatic shouts from behind. Lightning struck, called down by the hierophants. Bolt after bolt struck the giants but they cared not; nothing could bring them down, not might and not magic. The City Crusher was inevitable. It could not be stopped. It would swallow the whole earth; it would devour all kingdoms under the sun. Not all the armies in the world could stop it, nor all the powers of heaven. It was mightier than god.

OUTSIDE THE FHARESE CAMP, KORTHICA-THARTICA BORDER

Bat Zor watched with mixed pride and alarm as the City Crusher ground through the Eloesians' front lines. The unbreakable phalanx splintered as they ran from the City Crusher's spiked roller.

Her pride was tempered by the fact that the City Crusher was no Fharese invention. No, Mirzanēs—in his vast wealth—had hired the best inventor in the world. He had come from Korthos, this Agenor. "I can make you a weapon that will devour cities," Agenor had told him, "but there is no force on earth strong enough to push it."

But Mirzanēs had found a force strong enough—the twin giants Peor and Haamon, who had been raised from their graves by the power of the underworld.

Agenor had been delighted. He said he had designed a death ray and an "iron man" which he called "the Colossus" but lightning was required. Lightning from the sky was needed—not mere lightning conjured by sorcerers—and even lightning from the sky would power it only for a day or two. "At last," Agenor had told Mirzanēs, "an invention that will work!"

As soon as Agenor had drawn the plans, Mirzanēs executed him. That way, only Fharas would know the workings of the City Crusher.

As the phalanx broke, the Fharese warriors charged. The Free and Democratic Armies of Thénai and Korthos fled in panic; and Eloesus was no more.

SOMEWHERE IN KORTHICA

Days Later…

The heat of the burning plains had lessened; a few clouds were visible in the blue sky. Winter had set in. The nights had grown cold—and Ardyo had spent them huddled under bushes or at the tops of oak trees. He, together with a dozen men, were fleeing the Fharese army. The King of Kings had sent patrols of horsemen to cut down the retreating Eloesians. Ardyo had managed to escape their sabers, but the war was lost; he had failed.

Guilt weighed heavy on his heart: so many of his brothers-in-arms had gone on to the underworld. Now at rest, freed from the terrors and despairs of this life, they floated along the River of Souls. Now gloomy shades, their concerns were far from them. Ardyo still had to wake up each morning and think of the colossal failure of his nation. The terror at being cut down did not perturb him; the fear of death did not wear on his bones. The death of his nation… the betrayal by Hector… the willingness of so many, rich and poor, small and great, to surrender without a fight… that is what caused his heart to ache.

Having eaten the last of the roadbread, Ardyo and his dozen soldiers had to move on without food. Perhaps, soon, they would come upon a bean sprout or a farmer's field. At least they had water. Count your blessings, he had been told. But there were so few to count. Nor did he pray for the help of Amara anymore—her eyes were blind, her ears were deaf, her spirit was uncaring. Ardyo had brought her sheep, goats, chickens and even cattle—but it was for naught. She had abandoned Ardyo just as she had abandoned Eloesus. The priests were all fools.

Where Ardyo and his men now traveled, there were no roads—just gently rolling plains covered in grass and here and there a stand of holm oaks or a shady palm. The soil here was poor for farming, like much of Eloesus; it was too rocky and sandy. Eloesus alone could not provide enough food for its people; yet by ingenuity and hard work, it had created vast cities unequalled throughout the world. Too bad it was all fading—and the gods did not listen, nor nature. Perhaps Kyrion and the Korthian philosophers were right—there was nothing except the world around them, "nothing except us."

Having left their packs behind, Ardyo's men could move quickly. Their shields, too heavy to bear while running, had been dropped somewhere not far from the battle site. Thus, their vulnerability to Fharese sabers could not be exaggerated. If the patrols of horsemen found them, they were dead.

Following Ardyo's lead, they ran ahead. Ardyo did not know where they were. He did not know what had befallen Korthos. Surely, he could not take shelter there; not with Hector in command. Perhaps, there were no safe havens. Maybe he'd be forced to take a ship to the colonies; but the seas were thick with Fharese dhows. There was no place for him but here; nothing for him except death. Still he ran, toward an uncertain destination. Sooner or later, he would go to the grave, and join Mykalë as a shade.

~

Late in the day, when Ardyo was sweating through his too-heavy cloak and his body was covered with grime—when the sun had begun to dip low and the day started to relinquish its heat— there was movement in the distance, the sound of horse's hooves… a few dozen dark shapes. This is the day I die, Ardyo thought. How had it not come sooner? Why had he not died along with all those young men he had led to doom?

Would Mykalë recognize him among all those shades—those who had led such mundane lives that they were forced to float through the River of Souls? Perhaps his soul would not join her there. Perhaps—being responsible for the deaths of so many men—the goddess Amara would send him to hell and eternal torment. Mykalë, having lived a blameless but sad and short life, would face no dark eternity. But I will.

Ardyo drew his sword and his men followed. He hesitated and looked around. Behind him, he also heard the hooves of horses. Ten dark shapes were approaching quickly, galloping toward them. The closer they grew, the more visible they became—ten men, dressed in long southron robes, some with turbans and others bareheaded. One met Ardyo's gaze—his white eyes widened in delight and he drew up his saber. Ardyo turned to face them. Come hell or heaven, at least I will not see Eloesus fall.

Ardyo's men had also drawn their weapons—some swords, some spears. Tired and exhausted from their constant running, they could not hope to defeat these ten southron riders. But they would face their doom as bravely as they could—and cling to hope that they would prevail.

A storm of hooves erupted from behind; Ardyo could not turn to look before two women on white horses met the Fharese head on. They brought their glaives to bear on the southrons, slicing off two Fharese heads. The others panicked and galloped away, but not before one amazon rider hurled her glaive like a javelin and impaled a southron through-and-through.

One female rider watched the southrons flee as the other rode ahead to retrieve her glaive. The one who remained behind wheeled her horse around to face Ardyo. She was dark and black-haired, smelling thickly of perfume. A leather brassiere and a loin cloth was all she wore, and a buckler was on her left hand. Could this be true—an amazon, the ancient foe of Eloesus, riding in to help?

"On behalf of Queen Daphnë… greetings," the amazon said.

In the distance, her friend ripped her glaive out of the still-twitching southron's chest, then pierced him three more times until he was still.

"Amazons…" Ardyo said. Normally the sight of two amazons with glaives in hand and rows of chakrams around their forearms would terrify an Eloesian. But somehow, these were friends. Somehow, the natural order had been cast aside—and the amazons, with whom Eloesians had warred for generations, were joining hands with their foes.

The amazons were dark-complexioned, with luscious black hair tied with gold hairpieces. They wore no helmets, but over their chests were suits of chainmail, fitted for women's breasts. On their backs were oval shields, dyed green. In ancient days, the Eloesians had defeated the amazons in battle, but only due to numbers—the Eloesians, being much more numerous, drove the amazons from the mainland and limited their sphere of influence to the three great islands: Straiteira, Jogheira, and Agathë. Before all the nightmares with Fharas had begun, some in the Eloesian political elite openly speculated about invading the remaining amazon lands once and for all. It seemed like a horrid idea now, an idea which—if it had been executed—would have cost Ardyo his life.

"What is your name?" asked Ardyo.

"Aloë," she answered, "but that is not important. I can see you are dehydrated and malnourished. We have been rescuing you fleeing Eloesians from all over the region. I will take you to our camp—"

"Korthos—" Ardyo began, knowing not why—perhaps a

hostile place such as that was better than the world than the amazons.

"The city by the coast?" said Aloë. "It has been overcome by southrons. The queen is bombarding the city as we speak."

Ardyo had no idea where he was. He did not want to go to the camp—but food and wine would do wonders to ease his weary soul.

OUTSIDE THE KORTHOS HARBOR

Kora had been on this ship—this gold ark—in excess of ten days. Three of those had been spent anchored here, within easy view of the harbor. The gold arks dwarfed the Fharese dhows, which could not hope to overcome the amazon navy; but compared to the Juggernaut, the gold arks were ants.

The Juggernaut had been crafted in ancient days, and so many of its wonders were impossible to replace, for the means of their making had been lost. Once, the very sun had powered the behemoth as it sailed the waves—but the mechanism had broken, and now giant sails and teams of rowers had to propel the amazons' flagship.

A catapult was affixed to the deck—an incredibly large weapon of iron and wood which did not sink the Juggernaut. Now, loaded with stones via a crane, it flung a stone into the city of Korthos.

The sound of crumbling foundations and masonry indicated it had struck a target. Up on the High City—a mountain which towered above the streets—the temple lay in ruins. Its pillars had been smashed by the Juggernaut's catapult and the roof had given way; normally amazons refused to attack temples, but in such desperate times—when they were outnumbered by factors of hundreds—everything had to be tried, and every taboo had to be broken.

Queen Daphnë had expected the Eloesians to welcome her. She had sent Kora, together with a hundred handmaidens and a thousand warriors, to offer assistance to the city. But a southron had greeted her at the gates of the Long Walls—a man called Saana. Immediately Kora knew that the city was lost.

"We demand you surrender," she had said. "Vacate the city at once and your lives will be spared."

The fact that a woman had spoken so to Saana had enraged him beyond belief. He had called his men to shoot their arrows, but Kora's warriors had stricken the archers dead with chakrams. Kora had made an ordered retreat back to her gold ark; and the bombardment had begun, three days ago today.

In the harbor section, amazons had overwhelmed the southron garrison; the gate to the Long Walls had been burned away. The Fharese had sent all their men to take back the harbor and now—even above the sounds of crumbling stone—the sounds of clashing steel and shouting voices echoed.

The city would fall; but could the Eloesians forgive the amazons, who had destroyed their city? Its white pillars, its grand monuments and quiet arcades, had been bashed to pebbles. Was freedom worth such a cost?

GOD AND MAN

Next to his bones the sword did lay
The mighty Pyrax, green and bright
Next to the sword the helm did lay
The helm invuln'rable and true.

—Arkelaios

THÉNAI

Days Later…

He walked through Lion's Gate in nothing but a wingéd helm, a cape and a loin cloth. A sword was in his hand—a sword green in color, made of something like glass—but no shield. The people of Thénai did not recognize him, but they had seen his face before. For Theron was no longer dressed in the chiton of a government official, but instead the garb of a demigod.

The fire and pumice stones raining from the sky—the ash cloud which blotted out the sun and stole the air from people's lungs—and the lava flows which melted the countryside… those had not harmed Theron. The Helm of Invulnerability had protected his life; he had walked from the erupting Mount Kronos unharmed, even as the tiny villages were buried and destroyed. Billowing clouds of toxic gas had slain everyone for miles around, but Theron, wearing the invulnerable Helm, had marched steadily and safely away. The last vestiges of the demon prince Kronos had been wiped out; his dark power had been relinquished, and yet there was much to be done.

He had heard, on the way, messengers telling of the defeat of the Free and Democratic Armies. One passerby had spoken in terror of the Fharese, exasperated by the fact that Eloesus had ever dared challenge them. "Now we will all be killed!" the coward had said. "Our pride has put us all in danger…"

And Io, the sacred Woman on the Mount, had warned him of something else. The terrified archons of Thénai making preparations to surrender… and in Kersepoli, a full civil war that had plungéd the city into chaos.

Theron would make things right. Theron would make all things right.

OUTSIDE THE KORTHOS HARBOR

When the Juggernaut had stopped flinging stones from the catapult, and the sounds of battle were far-off and quiet, Kora knew the pummeling and bombardment had succeeded. This human city was a ruin; but the amazons had pushed the southrons out. They had destroyed all and called it victory; they had made a desert and called it peace. No doubt the Korthians themselves would despise the amazons for their "liberation"; their hatred would span generations.

Within an hour, the amazons had begun landing. Already a force of ten-thousand had been deployed in the region surrounding them. Now, the remaining fifty-thousand—amazon braves from Tigris under the command of Red Khloë, from Panther's Wood under Crazy Margola, from Ipsos under Reckless Reba, together with their sisters across hundreds of towns from Agathë to far Kalormenë—would fight the battle of the age. They were outnumbered, and they fought alongside Eloesians—but it was their battle to win or lose.

Kora was thankful as she set her aging feet on solid ground. She had grown too old for long sea journeys but—as the instigator of the war—she had a duty to see it to the end.

OUTSIDE KORTHOS

Two days after they had reached Korthos and joined the amazon siege outside its walls, the sound of crushing stones and crumbling masonry ceased. The gates of Korthos rolled open in a hurry.

Ardyo watched as—with panicked shouts—the remaining several hundred southrons fled through those gates to meet a flurry of chakrams and thrown glaives. How many southrons had died? A great force had been let in to Korthos; not a single one had survived.

A horn blew and Ardyo joined the charge as a stampede of amazon horsewomen entered the city. He ran in with the mob. Southrons were surely hiding inside homes, underneath tables and inside closets. Every last one would die.

At least the Eloesians would have this victory, before all was lost.

~

When Ardyo entered his beloved city, he did not recognize it. On the main thoroughfare which crossed it north-to-south, a giant boulder—flung from a ship—had broken up the pavement and sunk deep into the earth. Once-proud white plaster homes had become ruins.

Further on, the disaster became even greater.

In Heaven's Square, a boulder had collapsed the Temple of Tyros altogether and broken up the roof of the Temple of Nix. Bodies lay everywhere, and some women were weeping over them. The once-ornate stones of the square had been broken in three places, replaced with giant boulders.

Ardyo walked beyond Heaven's Square to find his home.

Entire neighborhoods had become rubble. At last he found his house—caved in completely. Could he forgive these amazons? Did he have the strength?

Across from his house was an olive grove where a philosopher had taught his disciples. The Academy, he called the area; and he handed out olive branches to whoever completed the course of learning. It, too, had not escaped destruction; bodies lay underneath the olive trees, and a boulder had knocked one over.

Ardyo examined the bodies, seeing slash-marks on their chest—they had been gutted by southrons. *No.*

In an instant, he was certain beyond all doubt. These dead men and women in the Academy had been slain by their own; the traitor archon Hector had sent his soldiers to slay them.

Ardyo put his hand on the cold head of a dead woman. He ran his hand through her blood-matted brown hair. What was her name? The flies had already gotten to her. No doubt she was a free thinker. Perhaps, the philosopher in the Academy had railed against Hector's treason. Perhaps, he had spoken ill of the southrons and their zealous fanaticism. Perhaps, he had denied the divinity of the King of Kings—and this brave woman had joined him.

He shut her eyes. "Amara," he prayed, "take this woman to where she belongs—the Fields of Paradise, where the heroes live."

~

In the afternoon, a light drizzle began. The amazons had begun piling bodies on carts—outside the city, a vast pit had been dug. The victory had come, but at a great cost.

Then, as the sunlight had begun to wane, Ardyo beheld a heartening sight—Hector, squirming like a worm, trying desperately to escape, was being hauled into Heaven's Square by the amazons.

"Please! Please!" he cried. He was naked and struggling furiously against the grip of an amazon. But his legs were cinched tight with rope, so tight that the skin bulged around it. "Please! I had no choice! I had no choice! I did not invite them in! I did not collaborate! I did not let them in! I had no choice! Please! Please!"

Korthian citizens had massed around him, outnumbering the amazons. "Kill him!" a man shouted and it became a chant.

"Kill him! Kill him! Kill him!"

When the amazon had dragged Hector into the center of the square, she let him go. Vainly he continued to struggle, but his wrists and ankles were tied. He could not escape. He continued to scream. "Please! I had no choice! I did nothing wrong!"

The amazon kicked him in the gut with a steel-toed boot. Hector's eyes bulged at the pain but the blow was so severe he could not breathe, let alone scream. Instead he flailed and curled up, like a baby, and wriggled like a worm.

"Burning is the punishment for traitors, according to our laws," the amazon said. "But we are guests in your city. What is your law?"

"Exile!" Ardyo shouted, but his voice was drowned out by the multitudes: "Burn him! Burn him! Burn him!"

In better days, civic loyalty was valued above all other things; thus exile was worse than death. But those days were gone. These days had produced people like Hector.

~

As the sun faded like a burning fire over the horizon, the amazons piled wood and logs into a great heap. Bigger and bigger this pile of wood grew, and Ardyo did not know why so much was needed. *Perhaps,* he thought, *it is an amazon custom—that so much fire is needed to atone for such a terrible crime.*

Then, when the amazons ceased their work on the giant pile and stepped back around the perimeter of the gathered crowd, a hundred struggling shapes emerged.

These were the demiarchs of the Korthian Assembly, all of whom had withdrawn their support for the rebellion after sending the city's young men to die. These were the traitors who had waivered in their commitments. Together with the demiarchs were their appointed men and women—there the Politarch of Water and Sanitation, there the Politarch of Commerce and Trade weeping into her hands.

They were all getting their due punishment, but Ardyo did not feel any better. Disaster awaited them all, one way or the other. All the amazons in the world could not defeat the monstrous human herd which the King of Kings brought over. There were too many southrons, and too many cowards.

One by one the screaming and wailing demiarchs and politarchs—together with Hector fastened to a pole high above to prolong his agony—were bound into their places. Amazons came by with jars of oil and tossed it onto the flame. Then, as the sun's light faded, it was replaced by a blaze which banished the night. All the roaring and crackling flame, combined with the cheers of the crowd, could not drown out the pained screams of the traitors.

Justice had been served; but disaster awaited.

HOUSE OF ASSEMBLY, THÉNAI

When Theron entered the House of Assembly, not a single face in the benches recognized him. Nor did they shout him out or demand he leave—their faces were transfixed. The astonishment in their eyes said, "This is not a man before us, but a god."

"I have heard that your commitment has wavered."

When Theron spoke, recognition dawned in their eyes. Hyron, Speaker of the Assembly, shot up from his seat. "Theron, you have returned… we have appointed a new archon. Polykrito! He is a good man… not as wise as you but—"

"Keep him," said Theron. "I have not come to take back my position. I have come to solve a problem…"

"Our commitment has not waivered," said Hyron. His expression seemed earnest. "But the other cities… Those, we cannot say the same of. Hector from Korthos has agreed to live on as a subject state of Fharas… to be allowed limited control of his city. He has let the southrons in! He has agreed to fall prostrate before the King of Kings and offer a white bull in his name…"

"An army—" Theron began.

"The army has broken!" Hyron's words spilled over. "The Free and Democratic Armies are defeated… There is nothing left. Not a one. Every young man… well…"

"No, not every young man." By law, the Free and Democratic Armies were voluntary. No one was compelled to serve. The generous pay had drawn recruits enough.

"We have remained committed," said Hyron. "Our archon has been drawing up plans. It seems we fight alone."

Theron had heard tales of the chaos in Kersepoli. Factions calling themselves the Lions and the Pigs had engaged in all-out civil war. Stranger stories had reached him still—of a "metal giant" traipsing along the Royal Thartan road, breaking funerary monuments and grave sites as it went. "It has terrified the Fharese," the traveler had said to his friend.

"I think there is little hope," said Hyron, "but as long as we are alive, the city of Thénai will fight…"

TWENTY MILES FROM KORTHOS, ROYAL THARTAN ROAD

The anger and hurt in Bat Zor had welled up within her chest. Her husband's betrayal was a stinging memory, one that cut deeper than a spear ever could. As the army set up camp for the night, Bat Zor—as she had at every possible time—left the tents to wander by herself.

She walked away into beyond the white paved road, and found tears streaming from her cheeks. No physical distance could separate her from her loathing—her hatred for herself, and for her husband's callous cruelty. Even now, he did not realize how distraught she was. Courtesans and junior wives she had endured like any queen; but the way he looked at that Eloesian woman in the red headscarf and loose white pants was something far beyond those. Love was far too strong of a word; but when he had beheld Bat Zor in the flower of her youth, his eyes had not even then looked at her that way.

Beyond the road were endless funeral monuments. Who would think of such a thing—funeral monuments along a well-traveled highway? The Eloesians were a strange people, of course; but this custom bordered on unbelievable.

The tombs and mausoleums varied in size and shape; some were pillared edifices flanked by statues. Others were merely immense tombstones. One tombstone bore a carving of a man baking bread: SOSTRATON, it read, HUSBAND OF HYDROMEDA, FATHER OF THREE SONS AND SEVEN DAUGHTERS. I WAS BORN POOR. HE WILL AMOUNT TO NOTHING, THEY SAID. BUT AS A BAKER I BECAME AS WEALTHY AS A PRINCE. I LEFT TEN TALENTS TO MY

CHILDREN. MAY ALABASTROS ACCEPT ME INTO THE FIELDS OF PARADISE...

Perhaps the road was chosen as a grave-site because it implied new beginnings. Perhaps the beautiful white-paved road was meant to usher them on.

How many lives were laid to rest here, Bat Zor wondered. Hundreds were within her sight, and the tombs continued beyond, up into the hills. She continued, sensing all the emotions which had left their imprints on this place—sorrow, grief, and more than a little joy. With the sun setting to her left, she wandered through this museum of lost lives, of men and women buried beneath the earth. The priests of Bel-Nohai and Nawäl insisted that drunkards and believers in other gods would burn in eternal fire after death—but as Bat Zor read these gravestones, she could not help but question it. Perhaps those who worshiped the old gods, like Thelema—devotee of Kronos—would suffer eternal fire... but what of "Lysander," whose humble gravestone included a hymn to Alabastros. What of "Helemnon," whose mausoleum spoke of his great love for his daughters? What of "Gyga," a seller of purple cloth, whose tomb said, I, CHILDLESS, HAVE GIVEN MY HOME AND ALL MY WEALTH TO THE TEMPLE. Perhaps Bel-Nohai and Nawäl were just different names for the same beings.

At some point in the night, after the sun had set, she looked back and realized how far she had traveled. The lights of the camp were far off, tiny and twinkling. The moon provided Bat Zor enough light to read the graves and their inscriptions.

Bat Zor's sojourn taught her of "Lydia," a dealer in perfumes and ointments; of "Kyrios," a farmer; and of "Nikator," a dealer in souls—that is, slaves. Who was Bat Zor to hate them? Who was Bat Zor to despise their country and their customs?

The people in the earth were far-gone; Bat Zor could not

reach into their minds and pry. Yet late into the night, as wispy gray clouds veiled the moon, she sensed the presence of another.

At the same time, the sounds of crashing metal and shaking earth echoed across the ground.

In the distance, far-off, the moon cast its light on a giant.

It walked awkwardly on its bronze feet. There was the sound of grinding gears and whirring machinery. Smoke emerged from a vent in its mouth. Its eyes gleamed in the moonlight. A jagged crown was on its head. Its chest was forged into muscles.

Bat Zor screamed and fled, heart exploding in her chest.

~

In the Royal Tent, where—of late—she had felt unwelcome, Bat Zor burst into her husband's bedchamber. Two concubines, dark-featured Zubaydi with fiery brown eyes, quickly covered their breasts with the sheet. The King of Kings, naked alongside them, glared at his wife.

When the wife of the King of Kings entered unannounced, it was customary for him to raise his scepter; if he did not raise it, the wife was to be killed instantly by the Royal Guard.

But her husband had no scepter, and no guards to send. Rage, however, was evident in his glaring eyes, his bared teeth. *My wife has grown bolder and bolder each passing day*, he was surely thinking. *I must teach her a lesson.*

"My husband." Bat Zor fell to her knees. "There is a giant… a bronze giant. It is moving towards us—"

Not a single word registered. His eyes burned wildly. "Get out! I will have you killed as soon as I am able…"

Bat Zor fled. For the first time, the sight of those two Zubaydi concubines wounded her. For the first time, she wept because of them. Her husband despised her. It was clear, now, that she was alone. She no longer cared for Fharas or for its mission; no, a victory would not please her. The thought of Fharas's defeat tasted sweeter on her lips, as sweet as the date-honey of Shakrath.

KERSEPOLI

Ten Days Later…

The gate of Kersepoli was shut, and from the city came the sounds of battle. Clearly, one side had won. It was Theron's task to mobilize those who survived. *One last chance for all of us… one last chance for all who remain.*

Lions had been painted on the street tiles, and on the walls of lean-to houses. Hoplites in full regalia stood there with shield and spear. On the streets were blood stains; in the city square a great heap of bodies was burning.

A man named Kleon had been elected king; he stood in the city square.

Kleon greeted Theron with a shout. "Here is Phillipidēs… who is ready to kill some southrons?"

The hoplites cheered. War was coming. *One last chance for Eloesus… one last chance for all who remain.*

OUTSIDE KORTHOS

After so much destruction, rebuilding the city's defenses was a haphazard, almost impossible affair. Where large gaps remained, Ardyo had his men reconstruct the stone walls where possible. But largely wood and earth had to be used.

The Fharese army had been distracted for days. The "colossus" which had sat idle in Korthos' square had suddenly come to life—perhaps by a miracle of Amara, or a lightning bolt from Arephon.

A spy had returned just yesterday, saying "An elephant has broken it apart; the colossus is gone."

And thus the battle of the age would take place here, in a ruined city. Every citizen, man and woman, would fight for Eloesus' future. The aid of the amazons had heartened him; but he had never been as certain of their coming doom. The southrons would make dark masters; they had no regard from their slaves. The slave markets of Nissos would be full to bursting with cargoes; and where would Ardyo end up? In some lonely desert, under an overbearing master? Perhaps he would fling himself off a cliff, or wander willingly into the whispering sands.

The walls had not been patched up to Ardyo's hopes, but a horn blew that evening, heralding the approach of the enemy. From the top of Korthos' towering wall, Ardyo could see far ahead—a dozen elephants with swaying trunks… and no City Crusher.

Had the bulky masterwork broken down somehow? Either way, the Eloesians were doomed. There were too many southrons and too few free men.

INSIDE THE COLOSSUS

The elephants had knocked off the colossus's hand, and the energy of the Cnidos Mechanism—which Pherion had believed to be limitless—had sputtered and faded. But still the colossus remained firm; nothing could topple it. The machine remained motionless, yet nothing could push it over.

As the lightning of the mechanism had begun to sputter and fade in brightness, the Fharese had sent in their greatest hope of stopping the colossus. A giant siege engine, it was—one he recognized, which the Korthian inventor Agenor had bragged about inventing. In height, it would dwarf even the towering walls of Kersepoli. A great roller with iron spikes crushed everything beneath it—soldier, horse, even the very earth. This had been days ago.

Knowing that the use of the death ray would be his last, Pherion had pressed the button. It had jammed. He then ran to the Cnidos Mechanism—knowing his doom was at hand—and struck it over and over. At last the energy burst into one last sizzling display; the death ray had fired, and an entire layer of the Fharese siege engine had vaporized.

The top had collapsed and the entire structure caught fire. Fharese soldiers flung themselves from the great heights, trying to escape the raging heat.

And the colossus had become motionless.

The Fharese army had continued its march—row after row, battalion after battalion, army after army. Thousands passed underneath the colossus's legs and around it for miles, each hour. And still it continued.

Pherion—safe though growing low on food and water—

now watched from his high perch in the colossus's head. He had seen countless men go by. Fharese soldiers had wicker shields and wore little more than quilted cotton for protection, but what they lacked in arms they more than made up for in numbers.

And the fair warriors of Fharas themselves were outnumbered by their subjects. Pherion had seen legions in full armor and crabshell helmets walk by; women leading tigers on leashes; archers on horseback with painted skin and dark eyes; together with beasts from the dark corners of the empire and slave-soldiers from a thousand nations.

And even now, four—or was it five?—days later, the ranks of the army had not thinned. Moment by moment, hour by hour, the armies' march continued. The Eloesians' doom was sure. Perhaps musicians would sing of the fallen nation in cities throughout the world. Or perhaps the King of Kings would blot their name from history.

On and on the warriors marched, thousands each hour. Their number could crush the entire earth; and Eloesus' doom was sure.

THE WALLS OF KORTHOS

Ten Days Later…

As the Eloesian and amazon lines began to falter, and ladders broke upon the walls quicker and quicker, Ardyo spared a hopeful thought. It was a wonder they had lasted this long, nine nights and ten days. Their faltering had only come with exhaustion. Thousands and thousands of Fharese had been slain, and the ladders—falling as quickly as beats on a percussion drum—had been pushed away or broken as quickly as they arrived.

The smell of smoke was wafting in the air. Ardyo looked to his left and saw that—despite the arrows of the amazons—the Fharese had at last managed to light the wood which had patched up the walls.

A ladder fell in front of Ardyo and he brandished his sword. He felt a pressure in his chest, looked down and saw the feathers of an arrow. He had been pierced. He staggered backward. Losing his balance, he plunged headlong and hit the scaffolding below.

INSIDE THE COLOSSUS

Ten days and still the army's march continued. Pherion watched as he drank the last of his water. To his horror and grief, he beheld a great mass of Eloesians marching in unison. These men hailed from the Ten Cities, but they spoke the Eloesian tongue and worshipped the Eloesian gods. It was at this point that any hope Pherion clung to vanished. If even Eloesians would join in to destroy the motherland, there was nothing left.

A MILE FROM KORTHOS

Every able bodied man in Thénai marched behind Theron. The hoplites of Kersepoli marched behind him, too.

The city of Korthos was burning, and on the High City, fire consumed the temple. The southrons had broken through the walls, yet the sounds of battle remained—a small fraction of the Korthian army remained alive.

Fharese soldiers filled the valleys and the hills like ants on a mound. Where once sheep had grazed in lonely pastures, now warriors packed every inch.

Was it a million or two million, or every person in the earth, who had come to conquer Eloesus? How could they possibly win? How could the Oracle set this task on Theron? Perhaps she was a liar, too, nothing more than a deceiver with magic powers—a madwoman with a hatred for Eloesus, with a great loathing for her own people.

"Forward!" Theron shouted. To certain death they would march. They would die free men.

"Forward, Lions!" echoed the Kersepolan king.

"Forward, Thenoans!" cried the archon.

Theron had brought tens of thousands of soldiers with him; but they were outnumbered hundreds to one. There was no hope— yet Theron clung to hope in his heart. *We will prevail*, he thought. "We will prevail!" he cried.

The Fharese took note of them and charged; and the battle began.

A Fharese giant in a great horned helm fixed his attention on Theron. He pitched back a razor-sharp cleaver and swung; yet when the bulky, oversized blade struck Pyrax, it was shaved in two.

Theron raced ahead and leapt up, striking the giant through the heart. The Helm of Invulnerability would keep him safe, for now; but its power was not absolute. A well-placed blow, and even Theron would fall.

"Forward!" he cried. "Forward!"

"Forward, Lions!" a chorus of voices answered.

"Forward, Thenoans and free men!" howled the archon of Thénai, dressed for war.

OUTSIDE THE FHARESE CAMP, TWO MILES FROM KORTHOS

As Bat Zor watched the burning temple on the High City, as she saw the smoke rising in great clouds like a demon from the abyss, a tear streaked from her eyes. She wept for Eloesus to some extent—a once happy and proud nation, a home to inventors and artists who had no equal in Fharas. But it was for herself she most wept.

A coldness greeted her whenever her husband spoke; all love had left him, replaced only with anger, bordering on hatred. She would surely be replaced. She would be lucky if she received a divorce; a demotion to subordinate wife was more likely. Who would he choose for chief wife, queen of the empire? Perhaps another harlot in a red headscarf.

She thought of herself as a young girl, wandering the Fields of Gilgamiel. She remembered herself picking flowers, filled with despair and envy and loathing. When the King of Kings had picked her as wife, she had rejoiced and praised Bel-Nohai; she had offered a white bull and a ewe lamb in his name. But if she had known it would all end like this, she would have wept.

Bat Zor ran back into camp. She would plead for her husband's mercy. All she wanted was to return to his love. If only she had not accepted the gift in the basket… if she had endured his affections for that scarlet whore. She had to make things right. She had to beg his forgiveness.

~

She entered the royal tent and the royal chamber without

asking. Her husband was seated on his gold chair, behind a veil. A warlord she recognized as Olim, a tall Rephathite, was conferring with him.

"Shall we kill all the men?" Olim asked—after, Bat Zor sensed, her husband ordered all able-bodied women and children be sold into slavery.

Silence followed the question. Olim turned to face Bat Zor, fixing his one good eye on her.

The rage coming from the other side of the veil was so palpable, Olim edged toward the shadows. Yet Bat Zor was not afraid; her own raged bubbled up, at years of betrayal.

"Kill her!" the voice of her husband thundered from behind the veil.

Sheepishly Olim drew his dagger. "Truly?"

"Kill her!" the voice shouted. "Kill her!"

Olim charged at her but Bat Zor ducked out of the way. She drew up all the power that remained within her and—fixing her gaze on Olim—took possession of his body.

~

How awkward was this vessel. From his eyes, Bat Zor could see herself, caught in a trance. Her husband tore open the veil, intending to flee. "Witch! Witch!" he cried, but Bat Zor—controlling Olim—caught him before he could escape.

Olim forced him to the ground, pinning him between his knees. "Mercy!" cried the King of Kings. "Mercy!"

Bat Zor could not do it. She could not murder him. She could not murder anyone. But as she gave up control of Olim's body, she filled him with inchoate rage—a rage which consumed every fiber of his being.

Having relinquished control of Olim, she fled the royal

tent, hearing the sound of slicing flesh.

Chaos consumed the camp. Bat Zor, weeping, found her black horse Midnight and mounted her. Then she rode off, a black rider on a black horse. She would never return to Fharas, or Shakrath. She followed the road as it went south, weeping for the life she lost and the husband she had left dying.

A MILE FROM KORTHOS

Theron's hoplites, locked shield-in-shield, were battling a regiment of Eloesian traitors. These folk from the Ten Cities wore Fharese chainmail for protection and bore Fharese scimitars and wicker shields. Archers in the back wore Megarine caps. Their lines were faltering. Their arrows fell uselessly upon the wall of shields. Some had begun to withdraw in panic; they were on the verge of fleeing.

Suddenly, chaos began to erupt in the camp far beyond. There were shouts: "*Emniyya Rephthaim!*" There were more shouts with indistinguishable words, shouts of rage; then the clash of steel against steel, and all-out fighting.

Like the snapping of the twig the Eloesian traitors fell back; the small bits of bravery they clung to vanished in the wake of growing panic. Theron's hoplites pressed on as a mass internecine struggle erupted within the Fharese ranks. The Fharese had begun to fight each other.

HEAVEN'S SQUARE, KORTHOS

From her place at the front lines, Kora—Solarine and proud amazon—sensed a shift in the Fharese ranks, and not to their own advantage. Beyond the front lines, battles had broken out between Fharese factions. The sight renewed her hope, and Kora fought with a new vigor, swinging her spiked club and flinging sunfire from her hands. The Fharese—having crowded each inch of Korthos' city streets—began to falter.

There were loud shouts. The ringing of steel echoed. Voices called out "*Afitar!*"—a word Kora had learned, in southron, meant "traitor."

The voice of Queen Daphhne echoed after them: "Forward!"

And with renewed vigor, the combined Eloesian and amazon forces burst ahead. The energy in the slashing of glaives and swords proved morale had returned. Somehow, some way, Kora felt victory was at hand.

A HALF-MILE FROM KORTHOS

Deeper and deeper into the chaos Theron pressed. The Fharese were killing each other. Their commanders were shouting and yelling, trying desperately to restore unity, but factions had formed. The tiger tamers had turned against the Fharese; the mahouts drove their elephants against their former allies.

It became clear, judging from their shouts of "Traitor!" and the chaos in the camp, that the Fharese king had been murdered. But by whom?

The Ten Cities warriors had already broken and fled. The lines of Fharese warriors with their shields and sabers had lost all organization. They were easy prey for Theron's hoplites, who marched quicker and deeper into the enemy's ranks.

Before an hour had passed, full-scale panic set in. The Fharese fled in a mob; and out of the gates of Korthos thundered a cadre of amazons on horse.

Amazons! If Theron's memory of Zoë had not been fresh, perhaps the aid of the amazons would have surprised him. But the amazons were good at heart. Of course, they would join the Eloesians against their oppressor; of course they would put aside tribal hatreds and go to war against an enemy much greater than themselves.

~

The Fharese had left their tents behind. The camp was ten times as large as Thénai. Over the coming days, they would plunder each tent. Surely the wealth of many kingdoms lay within.

But first, Theron had to see something for himself.

In the greatest of the tents, behind a flap, was a chair of gold, studded with diamonds, rubies, emeralds and sapphires. On the floor—bloodied and mutilated—was the man countless people across the world called a god.

Great gashes had been opened on his white silken robes, and the leather of the tent floor had soaked up his blood. He was scrawny, compared to his men. Hardly a soul had ever seen his face. He had ruled a vast empire, the likes of which the world had never seen; and now he was dead.

HEAVEN'S SQUARE, KORTHOS

That night, after they had buried Mirzanēs, King of Kings, outside the city, Theron—together with Kleon, King of Kersepoli, and Polykrito the Thenoan archon—made an accounting of their dead.

Of the Free and Democratic Armies sent, only two-thousand had survived. In Korthos, half its population had perished in the conflict.

"We will declare a day of mourning," said Theron. There was no joy in this victory. Korthos had been utterly destroyed; hardly a brick remained standing. The war had made many widows and orphans, from Korthos to Thénai, from far-off Nissos to high Arkadion. The great empire had been driven back; but in the ruins of Heaven's Square, not a soul smiled, not a person laughed.

Each city in Eloesus had been taxed beyond its limits; except Tharta. What had ever happened to Tharta?

OUTSIDE THE ROYAL THARTA GATE

Five Days Later…

Five days of hard riding, and Bat Zor's old legs and knees had not given out. She had rediscovered her equestrian Shakrathite roots. Yet she had no place in Shakrath. Nor had she any hopes of retaining her position in Fharas. The Council of Magi had long been suspicious of her; they sensed magical power within her. And in Fharas, "you shall not allow a witch to live." Mirzanēs' death at the hands of his loyal counterpart Olim would be seen as her doing. And then she'd be fastened to a pyre and burned alive.

The white walls of Tharta towered before her. The Royal Tharta Gate was shut, as should be expected in a time of war. Archers in blue capes were posted at the top with bows in hand.

"Let me in!" Bat Zor shouted. "This, I beg of you!"

"The queen has forbidden you from ever entering, Bat Zor!" the archer answered. "In fact, she has said, 'Shoot my mother on sight!'"

"Tell her the war is won—Fharas is defeated! Tell her I am no longer her mother, but her servant!"

Bat Zor did not know what to expect. Zubeida had always been rebellious. She had always cursed at wearing her *thawab* and stuck her tongue out at her mother. Yet she had raised a kind girl, a girl who cared for the poor and less fortunate. Could she ever forgive her donkey of a mother?

An hour later, the gates began to roll open; and Bat Zor, a black rider on a black horse, entered unimpeded.

~

A battalion of hoplites in full armor guided her to the palace. They had bound Bat Zor's hands behind her back with tight rope; they had cut the headpiece from her thawab so that her salt-and-pepper hair fell freely. A month ago, those things would have enraged her beyond comprehension. But now she was humbled; a common person in a great place.

Her daughter wore a gown that ended above the knee. A crown of gold was on her uncovered head. Her husband sat beside her on his throne.

Zubeida was glaring. "Cut her binds," she said.

Bat Zor felt the pressure of the ropes release. She dropped to her knees. She would beg if she had to. She would plead. Mercy was far more than she deserved. "Mercy," she said, "mercy."

"Father's war has not gone well, I take it…"

Bat Zor looked down. "No."

"And you come here, begging…"

"Yes," said Bat Zor. "I come begging." She dropped to her knees and began to weep. As the tears flowed she wetted her long hair, which had not been uncovered since she was old enough to wear a *thawab*. With her makeshift cloth, wiped Zubeida's sandaled feet.

Zubeida jerked away. "Stand up, Mother."

She obeyed. How radiant was her daughter, how beautiful, in her scarlet gown. How handsome was her husband, sitting beside her.

"I will have you bow to no one." Zubeida smiled; her eyes watered. Beyond the veil, behind the insolent girl, was someone who loved her mother deeply. "You are welcome in my court. You are a Thartan now… only…"

Zubeida signaled someone. Bat Zor turned to look and saw

a servant approach. He held a goblet of wine in his hands.

Without an order, without a word, Bat Zor—for the first time in her life—tasted wine. And it was good.

PORT JACINTHA, JOGHEIRA

Ten Days Later…

The gold ark moored to dry land. Spring was in the air and the flowers were in bloom.

Sometime soon, Kora would haul her old bones to Ipsos, to the Sun Circle, and give an account to her fellow Solarine of what had happened.

The war had been won; the remainder of the southron fleet had been burned; the army's food supplies had been cut off.

Yet Kora knew the limits of their victory. There would be no rebirth of the amazon race, no renaissance to take them to unseen heights. Their numbers had shrunken each generation; they remained a shadow of what they had been under the Old Dominion. Their decline would continue. Soon, they would vanish altogether. Amazons were creatures of another world, a world which had long ago passed away.

But Queen Daphnë had dallied near the shore; where was she? Where had she gone?

HOUSE OF ASSEMBLY, THÉNAI

Making love to an amazon was as dangerous and intense as Theron feared; yet now, with Queen Daphnë, he would never have it any other way. She was twice as strong as he was, and ten times as aggressive—making the sordid affair a battle rather than a pleasure.

Kissing her in this shadowy room, Theron remembered the long-held wisdom, that an amazon and a human cannot produce children. But they would try.

KERSEPOLI

When Pherion reached Kersepoli's square—haggard and worn—he was greeted by loud shouts. He thought, in that moment, that his deed was catching up with him. He remembered he had murdered Sardio.

But no, Kersepolan warriors in scarlet capes were running toward him, helmet-less to reveal their smiling faces. "Pherion the Lion! Pherion the avenger!"

In a city where the Lions had won, Pherion would be welcome. Of course, the brave succeeded where the cowards failed. The Pigs never stood a chance.

HEAVEN'S SQUARE, KORTHOS

Ardyo—who had led the Free and Democratic Armies—hobbled down the square on crutches. *Sad it has come to this.* He had lost consciousness in the heat of the battle, after the arrow had struck his chest. He had awoken that night as a physician ripped out the arrow with incisors. Such pain he could not forget. Such pain shook one's entire world. The memory of that agony would live on forever.

But now, as he hobbled to the well to draw water, he wondered if this agony was worse. When the arrow struck him, he had fallen headlong off the battlements. He had injured his neck and now he could scarcely put one leg in front of the other.

At last he reached the well at the center of Heaven's Square. He wondered if he had it in him to even draw the water out.

He stooped over—and out of his pocket fell a hyacinth.

The wilted flower had dried up and curled. It had been a gift from the Oracle, from the sacred Woman on the Mount. Some gift it was. It reminded him of Mykalë.

But there was another gift. Yes, another gift, a nonsensical saying. "Look to the mountains for your help," he repeated.

The words were so meaningless, so clearly mad. But as soon as he spoke them, he left the well behind. He would go to the mountains. If there was no help, he would call the gods liars.

~

Northwest was Mount Kronos. The mountain was too far; and besides, it had erupted in fire and smoke, and the lands for miles around it were smoking fields of ash. There were mountains close-by—ones he could see, southwest of Korthos. The peaks looked deceptively close; it would not be until late afternoon before he reached their base.

~

In the dark of night, he reached his destination. An inn put him up for the night for a very reasonable cost of two *thalon*.

"What are you doing here?" the innkeeper asked.

"Finding my help," he answered her.

~

The climb up the mountain taxed his frail body to the limits. When he reached the summit, the wind was bitter and cold. He walked up to the edge and saw, clearly, the city he loved, and the gleaming blue sea. "The gods are liars!" he shouted, and his voice echoed.

Then he looked down and saw the green grass. Trees lay far below—trees clothed in white flowers. Birds were chirping and pollen was in the air. Hyacinths, purple and red, blossomed amid the green canvas.

What a happy time spring was, when the hyacinths bloomed.

SUN GOD'S WHARF, THARTA

The war had been won.

But rather than join the celebrations in the streets, Demara had donned black clothes of mourning. Her husband Farhad had been enraged.

Demara had, every year, without cease, made offerings to the civic gods, but no longer. Eloesians were so haughty in their victory, so self-righteous. She would carry her loathing to the grave.

THE RUINED TEMPLE, MOUNT HYLEA

One Year Later…

The journey had not been easy for Theron, but he could not help his craving for wisdom.

At last, exhausted and panting, he reached the apex of the winding mountain path. The ruins of the temple lay still, but spectral drums were playing and satyrs were drinking on the lawn.

Like a panther the Oracle came sprinting to Theron. She fixed her sightless white eyes on her prey. She knew already the questions he had in mind. Would she answer them?

"You shall not have a child with Daphnë. If you value your life, you must quit her…"

Theron tried to speak but the Oracle screamed.

The snake was slithering up to her. "Ten dooms are proclaimed upon the world. Ten dooms and not nine; ten dooms and not eleven. The name of Thénai will be exalted for all time. Tharta will yet be brought low. But not now; not until the Shadow in the West rises and the first doom is born."

More madness, more insanity. He could not quit Daphnë; their love was more intoxicating than firewater.

"You have brought Thénai to its finest hour," said the Oracle. "But you will be exiled and come to despise the nation you saved. All these things have been determined, Theron… you cannot escape it."

Theron, she called him—not Phillipidēs. Had her opinion of him fallen? Or had he just been a pawn in her hands, which she had puffed up with grand notions?

"Go!" the Oracle shouted. "The Shadow in the West is

nigh; even now it is being born. Flee and save your life. Run to the southrons for your shelter."

Theron would never run to the southrons. He would never be exiled, nor would he despise the nation he belonged to. "You are a madwoman!" he shouted, finally. Everything he had done, he had done by his own hand. This woman had not helped him at all.

"Mad! Mad! Yes!" the Oracle howled. "Now run, before I devour your flesh!"

Theron walked away as the sounds of spectral drums and pouring wine echoed. The eternal revel would continue, high on this holy mount.

He would never seek the Oracle's advice again.

EPILOGUE

One Hundred Years Later…

"We Eloesians are scattered across the sea like frogs around a pond," said the actor. His masked form spoke the monologue to the audience in Tharta's Athra Fharseos Theater. "We are far apart and yet close. We are close and yet divided. We fight and go to war—we kill our own blood."

This play—"Lemnestra" by Quartillo—was one of the most popular. It had been staged every year. Thalasson—an audience member more often than he wanted to admit—had seen it perhaps a dozen times.

The world had changed greatly since Quartillo's day. Eloesus had become less a nation than a group of warring cities, utterly opposed to each other. Their successes on the world stage were not shared; instead they inflamed jealousies and caused each city to despise the other even more.

Fharas was no longer a threat, but a partner; and a common enemy had begun to form.

"We Eloesians are scattered across the sea like frogs around a pond," the actor repeated. "Let us pray one day we will see each other as one blood."

Murmurs had reached Tharta of a new power growing. Even Fharas had grown alarmed. Far away, in the land of Dys, nations were falling to a new Empire—a Shadow in the West.

CONTINUED IN BOOK 4, 'RISE OF A HERO'

To read more about the Shadow in the West, see "The Imperial Chronicles." Read about Varda at www.vardabooks.com.

GLOSSARY

FOREIGN PHRASES

Adwanīm: In Fharese, "heathens" or "blasphemers."

Emniyya Rephthaim: In Fharese, "Kill the Rephathites!"

CURRENCY

Thalos: A small silver coin, worth one-fourth a *doukos*. Plural *thalon*.

Doukos: The standard silver coin across Eloesus. It takes many forms but generally has the city's patron god cast onto the front and the victory laurel wreath on the back. Plural *doukon*. One *doukos* is about the daily wage of a skilled laborer.

Oros: A gold coin, worth fifty *doukon*. Plural *orhon*.

Talent: A unit of measurement, worth one-thousand *doukon*.

TERMS

Agathë: An island belonging to the amazons, located north of Joghcira.

Alabastros: The king of the gods in the Eloesian pantheon. He is revered especially by the Thartans. As king of the gods, he is considered to preside over kingship, leadership, and royalty. He is often depicted as a wise old man. His favored animal is the lion.

Amara: The goddess of motherly love in the Eloesian pantheon. In Thénai and the Amazonian Isles, she is also the goddess of wisdom and battle. Although a mother, she is a virgin. Eloesian legend states she is the daughter of Alabastros and the Earth. Her brother is Tyros, god of war.

Amazonia: A term for amazon lands. Amazonia encompasses the islands of Jogheira, Straiteira, Agathë, Kalormenë and a few smaller islands.

Amazons, the: A race of people living in the coastal islands off the Eloesian shore. Their women are far stronger and—some argue—more intelligent than their men. Though they look similar to humans, amazons and humans cannot breed. The child of an amazon and a human is always stillborn.

Architectural orders: The architecture of Eloesian public buildings and temples is divided into three orders. The most simple is Thenoan, with origins in ancient Thénai. The columns are bulky with a slight bulge; the friezes which run below the pediment are traditionally modest, with all likenesses heavily clothed. The Korthian order features ornately-fluted columns with curled capitals that resemble scrolls. No limits are placed on the friezes which run below the roof. The whitest possible marble is used. The last order is Megarine, with its origin in the Ten Cities. It is considered the most exotic and sensual of orders. The columns have thin bodies with capitals decorated in leaves and flowers. Friezes often have erotic themes to them; some Megarine purists say they *must* have erotic themes.

Arephon: The god of lightning, thunder, and storms. According to Eloesian legend, he is the son of Alabastros (see above) and the Sky. Hierophants are his priests. He is the most popular in the city-state of Korthos.

Arkadion: A village, the largest in the wilds of Themuria, called the Bride of the Wilderness. It is allied to Kersepoli.

Arkelaios: An epic poet, considered by some to be the national poet of Eloesus. He wrote a long epic poem about the Megarine War, a conflict between Megaris and its allied city-states (see Ten Cities, below) and the greatest Eloesian power of the time, Tharta. Arkelaios hailed from Nautilos and was said to be a cripple.

"Astromagia": A little-known epic about the life of Astromagos,

King of Tharta.

Baa'oul: According to legend, the demon prince of gluttony. Called the Great Slug.

Bajir: A region on Fharas's far eastern border, on the edge of the desert.

Barbarian: A non-Eloesian. The Isteroi and the people of the Ten Cities are often considered barbarians.

Bel-Nohai: In Shakrath, the king of the gods. His name in Shakrathite means "Lord of the Sky."

Bezakirah: A town in the Fharese region of Bajir.

Brecko: The god of wine, song, and theater. He is also considered the King of the Satyrs. He is pictured as a fat man with goat legs, accompanied at all times by his pet panther. According to Eloesian legend, he is the son of Tyros, god of war, and Seladora, goddess of nature. His sister is Nix (see below) whom he fears.

Cathay: A kingdom in the far east of Varda, barely known in Eloesus, considered impossibly distant and semi-mythical. The ruler of Cathay, called the Dragon Emperor, has established relations with the King of Kings in Fharas.

Chosen, the: The most elite Kersepolan hoplites, chosen by the king. Their number has varied throughout history, but is usually close to five hundred. As an elite force, they conduct special missions on behalf of the Kersepolan state.

Chiton: A knee-length sleeveless shirt, once popular across Eloesus but now restricted to priests and government officials.

Civic gods: The gods considered sacred to a particular city. Tharta favors Alabastros; Korthos, Nix and Arephon; Kersepoli, Tyros lord of war; and Thénai, Amara.

Courtesans: In Eloesus, the uppermost tier of all prostitutes—though all are considered low class. They are chosen by elite courtesans' guilds and taught—in addition to the art of lovemaking—the harp or lyre, as well as conversation. Because of this, they are often the most educated of Eloesian women, who are usually encouraged to stay at home.

Cyclops: One-eyed, cannibalistic giants native to Eloesus and its islands. Once widespread across Eloesus, they have mostly been exterminated throughout the mainland and now survive in isolated islands.

Demiarch: In the cities of Korthos and Thénai, members of the Assembly.

Devil's Chair: A mountain in Themuria, said to be haunted by dark spirits.

Devil's water: A term for alcohol among the southrons. In certain southron religions such as that of Shakrath, alcohol is forbidden or viewed negatively.

Dys: A land far west from Eloesus across the sea, on the border of the ocean, little known and little explored. Thartan settlers planted cities along its western and southern coasts: Mageios, Lornadion, and Agathion.

Eastrons: A term used by the Fharese and Khazideans, often derogatively, for Eloesians.

Elehoi: A large underclass, forming the majority of the population of Kersica. They are slaves, captives from Kersepoli's numerous wars, and all Eloesian by birth. The name means "little Eloesian" or "Eloesian-like."

Emir: In Fharas, a noble title ranking immediately below "king."

Faceless, the: In the Fharese army, the most heavily armored regiment, named for the helmet which covers the entirety of their face. They are chosen from youth, taken from their families and dedicated in training for combat. At any one time; there are one thousand Faceless. As soon as one dies, a warrior from the vast reserves is called up and given the specialty armor. Widely feared throughout Fharas, they are considered invincible.

Fharas: A vast empire, by far the strongest power in the world. It is ruled by the King of Kings, who is considered a living god. The word Fharas and Fharese also refers to a certain region and people—the heartland where the empire began.

Fharseos: According to Eloesian myth and legend, Fharseos was the founder of the Fharese Empire. The legend states his father Menarchēs was the king of Megaris. A priest of the god Alabastros once refused to grovel before Menarchēs and in response, Menarchēs burned the priest alive, destroyed the Temple of Alabastros and slew all the god's followers. In response, Alabastros cursed Menarchēs with madness and caused him to fall in love with his sister. It was by this union that Fharseos was born. In his disgust at the situation, Menarchēs cast the infant away to die; but he was picked up by a bird and ferried south to the lands now called Fharas. There, he became a great hero, slaying the Fell Lion and the Serpent Queen. He founded the empire in the Fharese heartland and eventually achieved godhood; his figure was placed in the stars, where he forms the Fharseos constellation. This legend is hotly denied by the Fharese and those who hear it are provoked to wrath, especially about the incestuous union. They claim the founder of the empire was named Fhareedi, a just and moral man of high birth.

Firewater: An extremely strong, colorless and harsh alcoholic drink preferred by the amazons.

Fields of Gilgamiel: A region of Shakrath (see below) noted for its springs and fragrant wildflowers.

Fields of Paradise: According to Eloesian religion, a region of heaven where the heroes and certain virtuous mortals go after death.

Free and Democratic Army of Thénai, the: The name of Thénai's army, composed mostly of everyday citizens. As part of schooling, every man is taught to lift a shield and march in formation. The army is led by a Stratego, or general.

God Manifest: In Fharese belief, the conception that the King of Kings is the manifestation of god on earth, and thus fit to be worshipped. He is not identified with any particular god, but is believed to represent them all.

Gold arks: Bulky ships, built by amazons, which have no sails. They are square in shape and propelled by several layers of oars. Designed expressly for war, their wooden hulls are heavily reinforced and equipped with battering rams. Each gold ark can house up to one-thousand amazon warriors, allowing for hostile takeovers of enemy ships.

Harem: In Fharas, among the Great Lords and high-ranking officials, the separate living quarters for wives.

Hierophants: Priests of the god of lightning and thunder, Arephon (see above). Magical talent is a requirement for entry into the priesthood. Hierophants are zealous devotees of Arephon, as well as wielders of thunder and lightning.

High city: A common feature of all Eloesian cities, a towering high ground—natural or man made—which serves as a fortress in times of trouble.

Hoplite: The traditional soldier in the Eloesian army. Each hoplite has a helmet and a breastplate, a spear and a shortsword, in addition to an iron-rimmed wooden shield. When fighting, he locks shields with his fellow hoplites, forming an impenetrable wall as long as he holds formation.

Ipsos: The second largest amazon town on the isle of Jogheira.

Isdar: The goddess of fertility and carnal desire. She once had a large temple in Tharta, where sacred prostitutes were employed. This was shut down in the reign of the Fharaizing king, Gygax I.

Isteroi: See Isteros.

Isteros: A region in the north of Eloesus, along the river Ister. The

Isteroi speak a dialect of Eloesian but are thought to be outsiders, due to their pallid complexions and frequently red hair. Arctos, the capital, is much smaller in size than other Eloesian cities.

Isle Men, the: A race of people living far west of Eloesus on a series of nine islands. They dominate the seas in the far west and are engaged in constant war with each other.

Juggernaut, the: The largest of amazon warships, designed in the square shape of gold arks but possessing many sails, as well as an on-deck catapult, a ramming device as well as numerous battering rams.

Kalormenë: The furthest amazonian island, west of Jogheira (see above).

Kersepoli: A large city, one of the four greatest in Eloesus. It is the most militaristic of the Eloesian cities and is ruled by two kings, either of whom may overrule the other.

Kersica: The region belonging to the city of Kersepoli.

Khand: A group of people who settled on the shore of southern Fharas. They are known for their often gold-colored eyes and dark, almost black complexions. They have worked their way up in Fharese society and have become top government officials and bureaucrats. They say their home is not Fharas but on an island far out to sea.

Khazidea: A kingdom far west of Eloesus, heavy under the influence of Fharas.

Kheroe: A land far west of Eloesus, considered the edge of the world.

"King of the Sun": A poem of Khazidea (see above) usually set to song.

Kleomenë: A port city on the northeast coast of Jogheira.

Kolkis: A port city on the southeast coast of Jogheira.

Korthica: The lands belonging to Korthos.

Korthos: A large city, one of the four greatest in Eloesus. It is ruled by an Assembly, elected by the people, and an archon, elected by the Assembly.

Korthian order: See architectural order.

Lake of Fire: Also called hell, this place—according to Eloesian legend—is a vast sea of fire and burning sulfur where those who reject the gods suffer eternally.

Laocon: A geographer from Nautilos who mapped Eloesus and much of the surrounding lands. He disappeared trying to find passage through the Sky Mountains.

Lion's Gate, the: The main gate of Thénai. Two lions are carved in stone above its giant double doors.

Long Walls, the: A series of stone walls which connect the harbors of Thénai and Korthos to the cities themselves. This protects trade and prevents piracy and sea raiders.

Lothan: According to legend, the demon prince of lust.

Magi: The priesthood of Fharas. They worship the god of fire, Athra, and revere all flames as sacred. Only youth with magical talent are chosen; they are taught both about the god Athra and also the skill of conjuring and controlling fire. Since magical talent is rare and can be found among the peasantry, becoming a magus is one of the few opportunities for advancement in Fharas's class-based society.

Megarine caps: A pointed cap popular in the city of Megaris, believed to derive from Khazidean priestly garments.

Megarine order: See architectural orders.

Megaris: A large city of Eloesus, the capital of the Ten Cities region.

Megarine War, the: An ancient conflict, shrouded in myth and legend, between the cities of Tharta and Megaris. According to ancient tales, the king of Megaris Sosimon fell in love with Prophylaia, the queen of Tharta. Sosimon abducted Prophylaia and the king of Tharta, Astromagos, declared war.

Megiddo: A vast plain to the east of Fharas, inhabited by tribes of horsemen. The plain is home to beasts of incredible size. Megiddi horses are among the hardiest in the world, capable of traveling long distances without much water.

Messenger of Death: In Fharese and Shakrathite religion, a servant of the gods which appears to those about to die.

Mina: The Fharese goddess of love, she is considered equivalent to the Eloesian Amara. She is a virgin, yet presides over mothers and families.

Mira: The goddess of light, especially sunlight. She is viewed as the creator of the sun by the amazons and especially the Solarine.

Molkoro: A jungle region in the far south of the world, considered dangerous and uninhabitable. Some call it the Dark Continent. It is considered to be part of the Fharese Empire, but no settlements have been founded there, only barren outposts.

Monotheists: In Fharas, a sect that worships the fire god Athra to the exclusion of all others. The more extreme followers claim he is the only true god and is locked in a struggle with Shemesh, the lord of cold, night, and darkness.

Nawäl: In Shakrath, the god of goats and agriculture.

Nautilos: A city-state in the east of Eloesus, far removed from the ocean. Once great, its population has dwindled vastly and now it is more a village than a city.

Nissos: A remote island off the coast of Eloesus, the center of the slave trade.

Nix: The goddess of secrets and whispers, her followers call her the Gray Lady or the Queen of Sorcery. She presides over the knowledge of herbs—healing and poisonous—as well as hidden knowledge, wisdom, and the metals iron and silver. She is feared throughout Eloesus, though her name is invoked for protection from the unquiet dead. Korthos was historically the center of her worship. Her favored animals are the owl and the dog. According to Eloesian legend, she is the daughter of Tyros, god of war, and Seladora, goddess of nature. She was hated by her parents and cast out of the household.

Old Dominion, the: A legendary empire which was said to rule the entire world. It was destroyed suddenly, in one night, by fire and ash. Its cities sank into the sea.

Otios: The first king of the Isteroi.

Phillipidēs: An Eloesian legendary hero, the son of a Thartan noble who fought in the Megarine War. According to myth, he was given a magic helmet by the goddess Amara which made him invincible to mortal weapons.

Politarch: In the cities of Eloesus, these are the government officials answerable directly to the Assembly. They are charged with certain categories of oversight; thus one politarch might manage the food supply, the other the water. In Korthos and Thénai, they are appointed by the Assembly; in Kersepoli and Tharta they are appointed by kings. Their duties vary from one city to the other.

Rephah: A people of the Fharese central plain and heartland (*Gor Ilan*), descended from a warrior of the same name. The Rephathites are known for their tall stature and their warrior traditions.

River of Souls, the: According to Eloesian legend, a river which winds its way through the underworld, carrying the shades of the dead. These shades, neither great and heroic enough to enter the Fields of Paradise nor wicked enough to suffer in the Lake of Fire, float through the river in silent sadness.

Royal Thartan Road: A road leading from Tharta to Korthos. It is the most heavily traveled stretch of road in Eloesus.

Saurians: According to legend, a race of lizard people which ruled a vast empire. They fed the people of surrounding civilizations to their god, a giant cobra. Stories state the amazons finally put an end to the legendary Serpent Empire and slew its god, burying the headless body deep underground.

Satrap: In Fharas (see above), a governing official appointed to administer a conquered region. The King of Kings appoints satraps directly.

Serpent War: According to legend, a war that took place between the amazons and a race of lizard people called the Saurians. It was said to occur in the years immediately after the Old Dominion (see above).

Seshán: The ceremonial capital of Fharas. The King of Kings has his chief throne here, but the town is inhabited only by his hundreds of slaves and government officials. Great monuments and titanic statues dot its streets. Its most remarkable feature is the throne—a mountainous work of stone with steps leading up to the apex.

Shakrath: A land in the east of the Fharese Kingdom, a harsh semi-desert region. The chief town is Umron, where the Shakrathite king also lives.

Shush: A region of the Fharese Empire known for its jungles. The empire's largest city, Taifun, is located here.

Sirens: Aquatic creatures which dwell in the seas off Eloesus. They resemble a cross between woman and fish, with green-scaled skin and a fish's tail. They can sing beautifully and entice sailors through mind-affecting scents which they give off, luring victims into a deadly embrace. Sirens—being carnivores—love nothing more than dragging a sailor into the depths to devour him.

Slavery: The institution is widespread in Fharas and offers slaves no rights whatsoever; they are viewed as objects or tools, not human beings. In Eloesus, the institution is banned altogether in Thénai and heavily regulated in Korthica and Thartica. Slaves have no rights in Kersepoli.

Solarine, the: In Amazonia, an order of warriors and magic weavers dedicated to the sun. Only women with magical talent may become Solarine. In addition to serving as religious leaders to the amazons, they have can summon gouts of bright flame— a flame so powerful it disintegrates everything it touches. They wear simple cloth robes and wield giant spiked clubs.

"Song of Fhardush": A Fharese epic.

Solar Temple, the: An open-air temple, shaped like a sun disk, which serves as the center of the Solarine order. It is also called the Sun Circle.

Southrons: A term for the Fharese, Khazideans, and more generally people from the far south.

Stratego: In the Eloesian military, a general or commander.Fsol

Stygian waters: Water from a lake in Thenoa (see above), which has long since dried up. The region was, in ancient days, called Stygia after the former city-state of Stygidos. A heavenly being was said to have died in the lake, imbuing the waters with its blood.

Taifun: The largest city in the Fharese Empire, home to the Order of Magi. Though Seshán is the technical capital, the King of Kings' palace and harem is located here; most government affairs

Ten Cities: A confederation of ten city-states, west from Eloesus across a desert, with Megaris as its head. The Ten Cities take great pride in their half-southron, half-Eloesian identity. They say they form a bridge between Fharese despotism and Eloesian democracy.

Tharta: A great city, considered the chief in Eloesus. It is ruled by a king but has certain limited forms of democracy.

Thartica: The lands belonging to Tharta. The region allows for extensive irrigation which results in plentiful food.

Thénai: A large city, one of the four greatest in Eloesus. It is ruled by an Assembly, elected by the people, and an archon, elected by the Assembly.

Thenoa: The lands belonging to Thénai.

Thenoan order: See architectural orders.

Themuria: A region of Eloesus, wild and undeveloped. Being at a much higher altitude than the coast, snow is common in the winter. The region's chief town is Arkadion.

Tigris: The largest city of the Amazons, having about thirty thousand residents plus half as many slaves. It is located on the island of Jogheira. The amazon queen, Daphnë, rules from here.

Tower of Stars: In ancient days, a tower which stood in the city of Megaris. It is named for its use as an astrological observatory. It was said to contain a device which could replicate the movements of the stars and predict solar and lunar eclipses.

Tyros: The god of war. He is revered in Kersepoli; yet he is viewed as never favoring one city over the other, delighting only in battle itself and spilled blood. According to Eloesian legend, he was the son of Alabastros and the Earth. His sister is Amara and his daughter is Nix, whom he hates. His lover is Seladora, goddess of nature.

Umron: The chief city of Shakrath, tiny compared to Eloesian cities but the largest in the region.

Zubaydi, the: A people inhabiting the South Seas region of Fharas. Their informal, pejorative name is the Sea Raiders. The islands in their control are called, collectively, Zubay.

ABOUT THE AUTHOR

Cursed at birth with a wild imagination, Andrew Cooper spent his youth dreaming of worlds more exciting than Earth.

He is a graduate of the Odyssey Writing Workshop. His stories have appeared in Morpheus Tales, Fear and Trembling, Residential Aliens and Mindflights, among others.

CONTACT THE AUTHOR

Visit **www.aj-cooper.com** to sign up for the newsletter and stay up-to-date on new releases.

Find him on Facebook at:

www.facebook.com/AJCooperauthor